Death at Tower Bridge

London Cosy Mysteries
Book 3

Rachel McLean

Millie Ravensworth

ACKROYD
PUBLISHING

Copyright © 2023 by Rachel McLean and Millie Ravensworth

All rights reserved.

No part of this book may be reproduced in any form or by any electronic or mechanical means, including information storage and retrieval systems, without written permission from the author, except for the use of brief quotations in a book review.

This is a work of fiction. Names, characters, businesses, places, events and incidents are either the products of the author's imagination or used in a fictitious manner. Any resemblance to actual persons, living or dead, or actual events is purely coincidental.

Ackroyd Publishing

ackroyd-publishing.com

❦ Created with Vellum

Death at Tower Bridge

Chapter One

"Bridges!" shouted the man in an accent so plummy Zaf Williams wondered if he'd fallen from a tree.

"No." The woman glared at him. "Bridget." She held up her phone and jabbed it. "See?"

Zaf shrank back as his fellow tour guide Diana Bakewell stepped forward. She had many more years' experience dealing with this kind of confusion and he hoped she could smooth the waters.

Although he hadn't yet worked out what exactly the confusion was.

"Can you show me the documentation you received?" Diana asked the woman, who was wearing a cheap bridal headdress.

"Bridget Jones tour of London," the woman replied in a Welsh accent. She held out her phone, an email displayed.

Diana nodded. "Yes." Her eyes narrowed: she was thinking.

Zaf frowned. He knew nothing about a Bridget Jones tour. The bridges tour, however, he did know about.

"Bridges," the man repeated. "It says so right here." He shoved a flyer in Zaf's face.

Zaf grabbed the sheet of paper before the man had a chance to do any damage with it. It was familiar; the flyer Paul Kensington, manager of Chartwell and Crouch Tours, had printed to publicise their tour of London's iconic bridges.

"That's correct, Sir," he said.

"Good. So what are these blasted females doing blethering on about Bridget."

Diana leaned towards Zaf. "It's a typo."

"A... a what?"

"A typo. Bridges, Bridget. The ad Paul Kensington placed on social media. He seems to have added a 't'. Possibly deliberately. Possibly not."

Zaf nodded. With Paul Kensington, there was no guessing.

"And we've got two groups booked on at the same time for two different tours," he said.

She gave him one of her trademark looks: surprise, mixed with impish delight and decisiveness. "We do indeed. And we'll just have to find a way to keep both groups entertained."

Twenty minutes later, Zaf stared out of the tour bus's downstairs windows as they drove along Millbank from Pimlico towards Westminster. Diana sat next to him, stroking the handle of her infamous duck-head brolly.

"If we were doing a tour of London's bridges," she said, "that would be fine. We've done stranger things. And I know for a fact that ACE Tours have been doing Bridget Jones film location tours for some time. Paul Kensington stole the idea from them, I'd bet my brolly on it." She waved the brolly, to accentuate the point.

Zaf grunted. Paul Kensington was the manager of the Chartwell and Crouch bus depot in Marylebone. He steered clear of the man as far as possible, and he knew that Diana couldn't stand him. Mainly because, for Paul Kensington, profit was more important than the customers. And much more important than Diana's beloved city.

He glanced round at the half of the group that had positioned itself on the bottom deck of the bus. "I'm not sure how we're going to get this to work."

Diana raised an eyebrow. "I'm formulating a plan."

Zaf grinned. Diana always had a plan. Sometimes – twice now – those plans had involved exposing murderers. But more often, they involved finding a way to entertain their guests when some daft idea of Paul Kensington's messed things up. Like that idiotic Londiniumarium. Zaf was trying to forget the Londiniumarium.

Diana turned to assess the downstairs half of the group. The contrast between them and the group upstairs was stark.

Downstairs was exclusively female, all of them wearing matching t-shirts with glittery pink writing scrawled across them: *Arwen's hen party*. Upstairs was a smaller group of men. A couple of them carried books about civil engineering.

Bubbly uncontained cheeriness and excitable chat radiated from the hen group downstairs, while the more serious and introverted group sat in near-silence upstairs.

"So this is all Paul's fault, right?" said Zaf.

Diana shrugged. After the chaos in the bus station earlier, she'd disappeared for ten minutes and he'd spotted her in the kitchen making calls. "The official story is that the poster in the marketing package had a printing error. Instead of saying *Bridget* in big, bold letters, it said *Bridge*." She gave him a look. "My theory is that our boss doesn't know about bleed areas when it comes to printing."

Zaf shook his head. He was a former art student and had dabbled in graphic design. "So the T got chopped off." He snorted. "A whole T."

"A whole T."

Zaf smiled. "Bridget fans and bridge fans. A unique combination."

"It should be an interesting challenge. Can we keep all the plates spinning and satisfy each group?"

Zaf tipped an imaginary hat. "If anyone can, it's us."

"It is indeed."

He smiled. They'd had some differences lately – over some *borrowed* shower products and an unfortunate incident with mistaken hash brownies – but he was glad she trusted him.

"Westminster Bridge," called Newton, the driver, from the front of the bus.

Zaf picked up the microphone. "Let's talk about Westminster Bridge, shall we, folks? It's the oldest of the bridges we'll be crossing today. It has seven spans and is a quarter of a kilometre long. What do you all think of the shade of green they painted it in? I quite like it."

Behind him, the women of the bridal party turned to look. They made small noises of agreement.

"Behind us now," he continued, "are the Houses of Parliament and Big Ben. Across the river we can see the London Eye. It's officially the largest cantilevered observation wheel in the world. Don't ask me what cantilevered means. I can barely say it, let alone define it."

A slim man in a paisley silk shirt popped his head over the rail of the spiral stairs at the back of the bus.

"It means that it's supported from only one side."

"Well, there we go," said Zaf. "Thank you..."

"Tom," said the man. He looked younger than the other members of his group and had a sparkle in his eye.

"Tom," replied Zaf. "We've all learned something new today. And learning new things is what a hen weekend is all about, am I right, girls?"

Another man, perhaps twice Tom's age, appeared behind him on the stairs.

"You said Westminster Bridge was the oldest bridge we'd be crossing," he said in that plummy voice. "But we'll be going over London Bridge, I assume? *That* is older."

Zaf drew in a breath. How to correct the man without annoying him? He didn't look like the kind of man who'd take kindly to being contradicted.

But Tom got there first.

"Stuart, we spoke about this. Westminster Bridge is older—"

"There's been a nursery rhyme about London Bridge for bloody centuries."

"But the current London bridge was built in 1973, so it doesn't count."

"The Romans built the first—"

"Different structure. Now stop bothering the guides."

"Knowing the ages of bridges," Zaf said into the microphone. "Very important." He waggled his eyebrows at the hen party and the women laughed.

Entertaining the hen group on the subject of bridges was one thing. He'd seen hip flasks emerging from a couple of tiny handbags and he knew this wouldn't be a challenge. But could he do the same for the men upstairs, when it came to the Bridget Jones locations?

Only one way to find out.

Chapter Two

As they left Westminster Bridge behind and headed for Waterloo, Zaf handed the microphone to Diana with a sigh.

"Two groups for the whole weekend?" he said. "With no common ground?"

"We can do this," she told him, eyeing the women on the lower deck. "It's all about the audience." She jerked her head upwards towards the top deck. "The bridge group are easy."

Zaf gave her a look.

She nodded. "We give them the geeky technical stuff, all the detail. It's like talking to Newton."

"I can hear you," said Newton, the driver, from the front.

"And I'm saying nothing about you that you don't already know," she replied.

"Then the Bridget group is like talking to me," said Zaf. "You want a bit of ritzy showbiz chatter or a fashion question to get them going."

Diana stared at Zaf. "Hmm. I'm not saying you're wrong,

in fact you're almost certainly right, but it does sound so very shallow."

"Shallow is my middle name," said Zaf. "Can't say I'm proud of that, but…"

"No," she replied. "You're doing yourself down. You aren't shallow."

Zaf pulled his phone from the pocket of his Chartwell and Crouch blazer. "Look at the content on my socials. Last three posts are about my grooming regime. Shal-low. How's anyone ever going to take me seriously?"

Diana leaned over to see stills from videos in which Zaf held up little pots of the products he was so fond of. "Is this a shameless attempt to get freebies, or a genuine desire to share knowledge?"

"It can be both of those things. D'you know what my most popular video is, by a mile? It was when I filmed Gus the cat grooming himself and then copied some of his actions to apply my own products." Zaf mimed dabbing his paw across his imaginary cat whiskers. "It was cute, even if I say so myself."

"The internet does love cats," said Diana. "But don't judge your whole life by the way you portray yourself on social media. I think it encourages shallowness by its very nature."

"Yeah. Maybe."

"You could always try keeping an actual diary. I kept mine religiously up to a few years ago. It's a useful way to reflect on things, as well as recording events and thoughts for your future self."

Zaf laughed. "What, like a super cheap therapist?"

"Diaries aren't always cheap. You'll see for yourself, on one of our Bridget Jones stops."

Zaf leaned over towards the hen party. "Bridget Jones fans! Who here keeps a diary?"

The party all looked to the platinum blonde bride, Arwen. Diana had identified her as a bride the moment she'd arrived for the tour. Not because of any kind of internal glow, but because she was wearing a tiara.

"It's such a nice idea," she said, "but who's got the time? It'd be fun to do it like Bridget Jones though, wouldn't it?"

"How d'you mean?" asked Zaf.

"Keeping tabs on her calories and units of alcohol and how many fags she's smoked. Sometimes it's like she's having an internal argument about why it's justified."

"I've never read it," he admitted.

Arwen pulled a face. "I think it's fair to say most of us here are fans of the film rather than the book."

"Colin Firth, woof!" growled one of the older women, in a low Welsh accent. There were laughs of agreement.

"We need to get some selfies," said Arwen. "I think it's time for bunny ears."

She rummaged in a bag at her feet. It was an enormous woven plastic bag, the sort that market traders used to transport their stock. Diana watched her pull out items of headwear and pass them round to everyone in the party, who put them on their heads.

Diana hadn't seen the film for years. But she instantly recognised the bunny ears from the scene where Bridget turns up to a posh party in a racy bunny girl costume to find that it isn't a fancy dress party after all.

"Could you take our pictures?" Arwen asked Zaf. "Try to get amazing things in the background if you can."

Diana met Zaf's eye. She held out a hand for the microphone. "Here, if I do some bridge commentary then you can get the London Eye in the background when we cross Waterloo Bridge."

"Lydia, get in here," said Arwen. "I want you next to me."

Zaf waved the women together. "Everybody, gather round that seat over there on the left-hand side, quick as you can."

Zaf arranged the women, ears waggling on their heads as they bustled around. Diana would need to address the other group upstairs. Bridget Jones hen party fun downstairs. Bridge tourism upstairs. It was an interesting juggling act.

She climbed the spiral staircase at the back of the bus to find the bridge fans near the front, pointing out sights to each other. She cleared her throat into the microphone and they turned.

Diana gave the group a smile.

"We're about to cross Waterloo bridge," she said. "The current structure was built during the second world war, mostly by women. It's a longer bridge than Westminster, coming in at three hundred and seventy metres because of its position on the bend of the river."

Diana glanced down the stairs. The bridal party were moving around the bus, posing for pictures. They waggled their bunny ears and leaned into each other while Zaf moved around to get the best angles.

She could afford to carry on with the bridge details for a little longer. She flipped open her phone for reference.

It was chilly up here. The men were all wrapped in fleeces and waterproofs, but her blazer was no match for the Thames breeze. She retreated down the stairs, microphone still in hand. The bridge fans weren't interested in looking at her anyway, as long as they could hear her commentary.

"I can't pretend to understand its construction from an

engineering point of view," she continued as she took a seat and gave Zaf a nod, "but I can tell you that it's clad in Portland stone, which is seen all over London."

There was the rattle of feet on the stairs and young Tom's head appeared. "Box girder construction is—"

"Tom! Later! Come on mate, there's views!"

Tom's colleagues lured him back upstairs. Diana shrugged. Surely there were more interesting bridge facts.

"This bridge was immortalised in the famous Kinks song, *Waterloo Sunset*. It's described as the meeting place for two lovers, Terry and Julie."

"Ooh a cat! Get a picture with the cat in it!" one of the hen party gasped.

Diana looked past her to see a tabby cat emerging from his hiding place beneath the seats. Gus loved to ride along on the tour buses and, it seemed, insert himself into photo sessions.

She smiled. How did a cat even know a photo was being taken? But Gus clearly did; since he'd adopted Chartwell and Crouch depot as his home a few months earlier, he'd enjoyed featuring in multiple tour groups' snaps.

He moved around the hen party group, butting ankles with his head and arching his back when the women reached down to stroke him.

"Gus will sit on your lap if you give him a bit of fuss," said Zaf, picking up the bus's self-appointed mascot. "Who's having him?"

There was a chorus of "*ME!*"

"The bride it is, then." Zaf placed Gus on Arwen's lap and settled him into place. "Stay there, boy." He continued taking pictures of the bride and her new friend against the backdrop of the vintage bus with its lovingly polished chrome and wooden flooring.

"Get some of me with a smaller group," said Arwen. "Negative space always looks good on Insta."

"You're not wrong," Zaf agreed.

Arwen pulled an older member of the group, the statuesque Lydia, in closer.

As some of the women relocated to different seats, Diana noticed that one of them looked tired and even unwell. Several arms shot out to steady her as she wobbled slightly. "Come on Gaynor, lean on us, we'll get you sat down."

"You alright, Mum?" said a woman with a slender cast on her forearm and a gauzy sling around her shoulder. Diana had noticed her getting on the bus earlier, but not realised she was related to another member of the group.

"Yes, Bethan love. I'm fine." Gaynor put a hand to her head and adjusted her hair once she was seated.

The woman saw Diana noticing the wig and smiled. "Don't mind my wonky hair. I'm not all that used to wearing it if I'm honest. Most of the time when it's just me and Bethan at home I live with being bald, don't I?"

"She does," agreed the young brunette with the broken arm.

"Not had a decent head of hair for a while now, but it's glad rags for my girl's trip, isn't it?"

Bethan smiled, and Diana saw the family resemblance. Bethan and Arwen were sisters, although without the clues, it wouldn't have been easy to spot. Bethan, like her mother, spoke with a strong Welsh valleys accent, while Arwen had smoothed the edges of hers. Arwen wore a low-cut top and tight jeans with full make-up while Bethan wore a plain skirt and blouse that made her look almost as old as her mum.

Bethan fiddled with Gaynor's wig, straightening it with her one good arm. "This this is all very exciting. But you'd normally be having a nap at this time, Mum."

Gaynor pulled a face. "I'm fine. This trip is just the tonic I need."

Zaf took some more photos of the bride then handed her phone back and plonked himself on the seat next to Diana.

"This is a group that likes its photos," he said, fanning his face in faux exhaustion. "I'll have my work cut out with them."

"Making the most of their celebration," Diana pointed out.

"Ooh, speaking of which, it's your birthday party in a couple of days!"

"Who told you that?"

"It's circled on the calendar on the fridge. Now *that's* a celebration I'm looking forward to," he said.

She frowned. "It's just a little barbecue in the garden square, not a massive blowout."

"What? You want me to cancel the stripogram?"

"You haven't?" She gave him a shrewd look. "Have you?" He raised an eyebrow and she decided he was kidding her. "Sometimes, I think nothing is beyond you, Zaf Williams. But if you do bring a stripogram to my birthday, I will have no choice other than to murder you."

Chapter Three

Zaf was looking forward to Diana's birthday party, and wanted to find a way to make it extra special. She'd let him live in her house, and after a few fallings-out over minor issues, they were getting along well. Every once in a while, when he stopped to think about it, Zaf would boggle at the enormity of her kindness. Living anywhere in London was expensive, but Eccleston Square was in a league of its own, and Diana seemed happy to share her flat there with him.

They were on the dual carriageway running along the north bank of the Thames, Somerset House on he left and Blackfriars Bridge up ahead. "Do you have any favourites we haven't included on the food list for the barbecue?" he asked her.

"We've spoken about this," she replied. "It's in hand. We'll have plenty of whatever we need."

He shrugged. "Fine. That's good then."

"Trust me. I've a sight more experience of birthdays than you do."

Zaf raised an eyebrow. "Would you care to tell me how many birthdays?"

"I'm not embarrassed, but it's not important. And if you really wanted to know, you'd find out."

Zaf's best guess was that there was something like forty years between them. He was twenty-one. Diana didn't actually look like she was in her sixties, but she seemed to have the wisdom and self-confidence of a woman who'd been around for centuries. The age gap had caused some tour guests to wonder if they were mother and son, an idea which would have amused Zaf's St Lucian mum in Birmingham.

Zaf had two more days to come up with a way to blow Diana's socks off on her birthday. He was sure he'd think of something, but so far, he couldn't seem to find the one brilliant idea that would make a triumph of the night. He just had to dig a little deeper.

The bus trundled along Lower Thames Street, separated from the river by converted warehouses and sleek office buildings. A modern bus was in front of them, stopping at every bus stop and making him wonder why members of the public never tried to get on their Routemaster.

One of the bridge group called down the stairs.

"It's starting to rain!"

"Tourist complaining about the British weather again," said Diana,

"I'll pop up and check they're alright." Zaf didn't want them to think that they were being ignored.

He went upstairs. The group of men had turned their collars up against the spattering rain. One of them had hunkered down, intent on the book in his hand, as if he could make the rain go away by simply ignoring it. The droplets felt refreshing on Zaf's face.

"You're skipping some of the bridges," grumbled a well-spoken man in a tweed jacket. Zaf thought back: yes, that was Stuart, the one who'd insisted London Bridge was the oldest.

"We're not skipping them, Sir," Zaf said. "We're saving them for another time."

The younger guy, Tom, who was cute despite an obvious passion for bridges and knowledge of words like *cantilevered*, made a silly face at Zaf.

"You don't even care for bridges, Stuart," he said.

"I just want to know I'm getting my money's worth." Stuart shook the tourist map in his hand. "Blackfriars, the Millennium Bridge, Southwark Bridge, London Bridge. Passed them all. If we don't get to drive over them at some point..."

"Might be tricky with the Millennium Bridge," Zaf said, "as it's pedestrian."

"That's the Wobbly Bridge," Tom said, looking around his companions. "You know the one. Started swaying dramatically when it opened as a result of synchronous lateral excitation."

Stuart looked at Zaf. "Is that really true?"

"The synchronous lateral... um?"

"Excitation?"

"I say," said a man in the seat behind, "is that the one that the Death Eaters destroyed in the Harry Potter film?"

Zaf looked at him. He'd thought Stuart was well-spoken, but Stuart had nothing on this guy. He was ruddy-faced with wispy hair and the voice of someone born with the proverbial silver spoon in his mouth.

But at least he'd asked a question Zaf could answer.

"Yes," he said. "Through the power of special effects the

wobbly Millennium Bridge was destroyed at the beginning of the, um... fifth?... Harry Potter film."

"I bally well love Harry Potter, I do."

Zaf resisted a raised eyebrow. *Bally?* Did people really say that?

"I'll point out any other famous Potter locations as we proceed," he said. "But, for now, we're going straight to Tower Bridge. We've arranged to go inside after we've paused to pick up our Colin Firth lookalike and had a stop for lunch."

"Colin Firth?" said the man hunched over his paperback book.

"He was in Bridget Jones," said the *bally* one.

A grunt.

"But what about the rain?" asked Stuart, looking at Zaf as if he expected tour guides to have powers over the weather.

Zaf gestured at the small cowl-like roof covering the front seats of the open-top bus. "You could squash up in there."

"The views aren't as good," said Stuart.

"That's why we're still sitting here in the rain," said the book-reader. "We're in a great position to observe fine bridge detail."

The man was so intent on his book that Zaf wasn't sure how much detail he was actually capable of observing.

"I can see the attraction," Zaf said. "But you're very welcome to come downstairs if the weather deteriorates."

Tom gave Zaf a mock-serious look. "I hear that hen parties can be raucous."

"They're just women," scoffed the *bally* one, "not a dangerous foreign tribe."

Tom looked at his posh friend. "Bunty, you may be right. But before we undertake the trip into *terra incognita*, perhaps our delightful tour guide can assure us we'll be safe in the strange land below."

The other men rolled their eyes. Zaf grinned. "Well, bold traveller. You'll be pleased to hear that the climate downstairs is drier than it is up here, and the locals are friendly."

The bus came to a halt by Tower Hill Gardens. In front of them were two hop-on, hop-off tour buses and behind them a red London bus, significantly more modern than their own vintage Routemaster.

Zaf peered over the side of the bus to see a man approach, wearing a fitted suit. From above, he might have passed as a younger Colin Firth.

There was a gust of wind, blowing rain into the men's faces.

"Come on," Zaf said. "I think we should go downstairs."

He led the way towards the stairs. As the women of the hen party turned to look at the slightly bedraggled men descending, Zaf gave them a grin.

"Whohoo!" He turned and made a gesture, encouraging the men to copy him.

"Whohoo!" hollered Tom, and Zaf's smile broadened. The other men shuffled down in gruff embarrassment, barely looking at the women.

"For goodness sake, Tom!" said posh Bunty. "Don't overdo it! You'll give the women the entirely wrong idea about you."

Zaf's eyes met Tom's. He could sense that the other man was resisting a laugh, too.

Zaf pulled back his shoulders and gave Bunty a grave look: *professional*.

"Don't worry," he said. "I'm sure we'll be perfectly safe. They're women, not savage killers."

Chapter Four

Diana greeted the newcomer as he stepped onto the bus's rear open platform and shook the rain from his sleeves. At the same moment, a second man hurried across three lanes of road and hopped on.

He gave her an apologetic grin. "Sorry! I didn't know which direction you'd be coming from."

The rear platform of the bus was crowded with bridge afficionados making their way down from the upper deck. Diana shifted to get out of their way and addressed the two new arrivals.

"Does one of you have a contract for the day with Chartwell and Crouch?"

"Yes," they chorused, then looked at each other.

She frowned. "You can't both have the contract. We booked a Colin Firth lookalike."

"That's me!" said one.

The other pointed to himself. "I'm the number one Colin Firth lookalike in London."

The two of them looked each other up and down.

"Are we OK to go?" Newton called from the front.

Diana would have to sort this out on the move. "I suppose so..."

The two Firth-a-likes were an interesting sight. Each of them bore some obvious similarities with the actor. The one who'd claimed to be 'number one in London' had Colin's deep and penetrating blue eyes. The other had his well-defined, expressive eyebrows. One had the masculine jawline and healthy complexion, while the other had the well-proportioned nose and the warm smile.

Between them, they definitely made up at least one and a half perfect Colin Firths.

The two Firth-a-likes continued to look one another up and down with undisguised contempt. One of them reached out and flicked the sideburns of the other. "Seriously. Those things aren't even real."

"That's because I do Piers Morgan at the weekends."

A scowl. "You can't be *both*."

"It's called having *range*. I'm not a one trick pony."

The first raised his fingers in air quotes. "I *actually* look like Colin Firth, I don't just practise pouting and smouldering in the mirror."

Diana glanced over at Zaf, who looked simultaneously horrified and gleefully entertained. He kept glancing towards a slim man in a beautiful paisley shirt. The man was laughing and chatting with some of the women.

Diana noticed Gaynor, the mother of the bride, placing a hand on her other daughter's arm cast. She was looking into the younger woman's eyes, her brow furrowed.

"I just don't want you to get hurt," she said.

Diana glanced at Bethan's cast. It looked like it was too late, in one sense at least.

She looked around the bus. With both groups downstairs now and the two Colin Firths having joined them, the space was crowded. She couldn't tell how many people there were down here.

"Zaf," she called to him past the Firth-a-likes, "did all the bridge party come down with you?"

He looked around the groups. "I think so."

The two Colins were still arguing. She inserted herself between them and put up her hands for them to stop.

"I don't know what's gone wrong with the booking, but I do know that whatever's going on between the pair of you, I won't allow it to affect my clients. Now if one of you wants to leave, this is the time. Otherwise, I suggest you both take a seat and work it out as we drive."

The two men gave each other a final hard stare. Then they both, as one, pulled out their phones.

Diana shook her head.

"Zaf," she called, "tell Newton—"

Zaf turned towards the front of the bus. "Let's go, mate."

Newton raised a hand and the bus began to move. Diana could only hope that as far as the hen party were concerned, two Firths would be better than one.

There was a ripple of laughter from the Bridget Jones group as one of the bridge men pointed out the Colin Firths.

Zaf was in the middle of the hen party, chatting to them as they passed Gus between their laps.

"Is this the best thing ever?" he said. "It's like you're actually Bridget Jones, with two men fighting over you all."

Diana glanced at the Firths. Fake Sideburns was talking into his phone.

"Claude? Claude! There's been a cock-up. I've come to do the Chartwell and Crouch job and that other guy's here too." A pause. "What d'you mean, which one? How many Colin Fi… did you say seven? Seven Colin Firths? Oh."

Real Sideburns was muttering into his phone. "Claude, it's me. Look, I'm not happy with this treatment. If this happens again, I'll—"

He spotted Diana watching him and cupped his hand around the phone. After a moment he slid the phone into his inside pocket. Diana had to admit, there was something about the movement that did remind her of Colin Firth.

Fake Sideburns was still talking.

"No, of course I haven't been acting up in front of the client. I'm a professional, you know that. I can't speak for the other—"

"You tell Claude that he knows I'm the perfect professional," interrupted Real Sideburns.

Fake Sideburns ignored him. "Uh-huh. No. I understand. Well, I'm just saying this treatment is unacceptable."

"Is that the booking agent?" Diana said. "Can I speak to him?"

Fake Sideburns looked at her for a moment, then handed over his phone.

She spoke into the phone, both men watching her. Fake Sideburns was starting to look contrite. She stifled a smile.

"Thanks, Claude," she said at last. "I'm grateful."

She handed the phone back to Fake Sideburns.

"Right," she said. "I know Claude of old. He said two things. First, he says you can both work this gig at no extra cost to us."

She looked at Zaf, who shrugged. "I think we can make use of two Colin Firths."

She nodded, looking back at the Firth-a-likes. "He also said that he'd be prepared to pay you both, as a gesture of goodwill, but only if the feedback from the client is that you've conducted yourselves well and not acted like a pair of squabbling children."

The two men looked at each other. Fake Sideburns wrinkled his nose.

Diana waited.

The men nodded. Real sideburns put out a hand and his rival shook it.

Thank goodness for that.

"Good," she said. The bus was passing the Tower of London, with Tower Bridge looming beyond it.

"Always handy to have a spare Colin Firth." Zaf shrugged. "You know, in case one of them dies or something."

Chapter Five

Zaf took a seat next to one of the bridge men. This one was dressed in tweed from head to toe: Stuart, Zaf remembered.

"I've got to ask," Zaf asked him. "How did the group decide to go on a tour of London bridges. Did you all know each other beforehand?"

Stuart sighed. "Tom there is my cousin – my much younger cousin. The bridge thing was really his and Bunty's idea. I only came in to offer some sanity and initial collateral."

"Collateral?"

"I'm in plants," said Stuart.

"Are you?" Zaf was none the wiser.

"Stuart Dinktrout, as in the Dinktrout Rose. A beautiful variety. My main nursery is in Suffolk. Tom and Bunty go way back. University? School?"

"First year at St John's," Bunty called out. "Well, he was first year, I was... the less said about that, the better. This weekend is a combination of business and pleasure. For some of us, it's the first time we've met. Who knew that tour companies did bridge-specific tours, eh?"

He was having to raise his voice to be heard, as the women were getting more and more raucous in their appreciation of the Colin Firths. Zaf couldn't help but notice that the Colins seemed to be sulking.

"Where do you want us?" one of the lookalikes asked Diana.

She wafted a hand towards the hen party group. "These ladies here are celebrating Arwen's forthcoming wedding. They're Bridget Jones fans and I'm sure they'd love some selfies."

Fake Sideburns patted his hair and face. "I wonder if I could transform myself into Hugh Grant? That would make for some quality photos."

Zaf watched him tousle his hair and bury his face in his hands, the process accompanied by strange chanting sounds.

"What's he saying?" Diana muttered.

"No idea." He was mumbling some sort of incantation.

Real Sideburns raised an eyebrow. "I do believe he is telling himself that he is charming, handsome and shallow, in the belief that it will make him more like Hugh Grant."

Zaf laughed. He hadn't been born when the film came out, but it was one of his sister Connie's favourites. He knew the characters well.

Fake Sideburns blew out a breath and lifted his head. He gave a lazy smile and looked around at his audience: Bridget Jones fans and bridge fans.

"Good grief," he said, "it's hard work being this English. Who here minds if I swear? Swearing is effing glorious isn't it?"

Zaf leaned in towards Diana, shifting out of the way for

one of the bridal party to take a photo. "He's done it. Somehow, he actually looks like Hugh Grant."

Diana nodded. She picked up the microphone. "We have something for everyone now. Colin Firth and Hugh Grant are here."

There was a cheer from the hen party.

She looked out of the window. "And we're about to cross the iconic Tower Bridge. Right now."

Zaf turned to see they were on the approach to Tower Bridge. He reminded himself that it wasn't just the hen party on this tour.

He cleared his throat and spoke into the microphone. "Over there, you'll see the traffic lights that turn red if the bridge needed to open for a ship to pass through."

A ripple of conversation ran through the men. Both parties turned to look out of the bus as they drove over the bridge.

Zaf watched them pointing and muttering. Tower Bridge was such an ornate structure, as famous a symbol of London as Big Ben or Buckingham Palace. It was easy to forget that it was a functioning bridge that carried tens of thousands of tons of traffic every day.

"Someone get one of me with the bridge in the background!" called Arwen to her hens. She gestured for Colin Firth and Hugh Grant to stand either side of her and smiled for the camera. Zaf fired off some pictures, twisting to get close while everyone moved around. Gus somehow managed to insert himself into nearly every shot.

As Zaf was taking one of Arwen holding Gus up to be stroked by Hugh Grant, there was a loud thumping sound.

Zaf whipped round. Had he knocked something over?

"Anyone hear that?"

Nobody replied.

He looked out. They were driving across the main span of the bridge. Twin walkways passed overhead from the north towers to the south.

He shook his head: he'd been imagining things.

"It's cleaner than I expected." Gaynor, the mother of the bride, was staring out of the window. "The stonework, I mean. Doesn't the smog stain it?"

"I don't think they have smog in London anymore," Zaf replied.

"No," she said. "Before your time and mine, I suppose."

"The views from the top are amazing," he said.

"Oh, I'm not sure how I'd get on with those heights."

"In that case, I won't tell you that the walkways up there have glass floors."

She put a hand on her heart. "No, you won't."

The bus trundled off the bridge on the south side of the river and, edging around each other, the members of both groups finished taking their photos and found themselves places to sit. Hugh Grant and Colin Firth had ended up at the back of the bus, near Zaf and Diana.

Diana gave Zaf a smile. "You know you want to."

He gave a wide grin and stood between the two men. He pulled his best Bridget Jones face and pouted for anyone who would take his picture while the bus took them round Tooley Street and Druid Street, and into the heart of Southwark.

As he thanked the two lookalikes, he felt a tap on his shoulder and turned to see Stuart standing behind him.

"I thought we were going to have a look around the bridge."

"After lunch," Diana told him. "We're stopping at the Globe Tavern. Some of our eagle-eyed guests will recognise it as the exterior location of Bridget's bachelorette pad in the first film."

He grunted. Zaf could sympathise; the rain meant they weren't exactly getting the best view of the bridges.

Even in the drizzle, the pavements along Borough High Street were crowded with shoppers. The bus passed beneath railway bridges and high buildings, the urban landscape seeming to close in.

Newton stopped the bus on Bedale Road, just along from The Globe Tavern.

Zaf nodded in approval. The pub was a proper, old-fashioned-looking London boozer. He could imagine the workers from Borough market coming here for a pint a hundred years ago.

"I'll check for stragglers upstairs," said Diana, "and then we'll get them all inside."

Zaf leaned out of the back of the bus and peered up at the sky as Diana ascended the stairs. It was brightening.

"Zaf," Diana called. "Can you get up here?"

Diana rarely shouted, but she had a way of speaking when something wasn't right. Zaf could hear that tone in her voice now.

He raced up the steps, stumbling as he tried to take them two at a time.

"What's wrong?" he panted as he reached the top.

Diana was towards the front of the bus, her back to him. She was bending over.

He stepped towards her. "Diana?"

She crouched down. He took another step forward and realised there was a man on the floor beside her.

Diana picked up the man's wrist, checking his pulse. Zaf felt his breath catch.

The man was laid out on his front on the floor. His suit was soaked through from the rain and his hair was plastered to his temple, where there was a large and angry bruise.

"I need to call the emergency services," Diana said.

"Is he alright?" Zaf asked, knowing it was a stupid thing to say.

A raindrop splashed on Diana's cheek, but she didn't seem to notice.

"He's dead," she said.

Chapter Six

Diana stood, her mind racing.

She prided herself on being the sort of person who knew what to do in a crisis, but this was a crisis beyond even her imagining.

She'd come across dead bodies before, of course.

But not on the bus. Never on the bus.

The first step had to be calling the emergency services. But then what to do with the guests?

There was a man on the top deck of the bus. Dead. And she didn't even know who he was.

"I was sure everyone had gone downstairs." Zaf's voice was hollow.

Diana nodded. She put a hand on his arm and took out her phone to dial 999.

"I did hear a thump while we were crossing Tower Bridge," he said. "You don't think...?"

She looked at him. "I don't think what?"

Using his fingers to imitate the legs of a walking man, Zaf

mimed a figure falling from a height and hitting the palm of his hand. "Onto the open top bus." He swallowed.

Diana frowned. Never mind how the man got here. They had a situation to deal with. Customers to manage.

Zaf looked into her face, then stood up. "I'll take the people downstairs into the Globe. I won't tell them anything. But I'll let Newton know."

She sighed. At last, he was on her wavelength. "Do a headcount," she said.

"Right." Zaf disappeared downstairs and Diana hit the call button.

"999 emergency, please state the nature of the emergency."

"I've found a body. He's dead." She looked down at the man. "I'm mostly sure he's dead."

"OK. Give me your details and we'll send help."

Diana gave the woman her location and relayed what she could of the man's condition. As she spoke, she heard Zaf and the tourists leaving the bus. He'd clearly managed to avoid conveying his shock, as the dominant noises from below were laughter and loud conversation. Two men were arguing about suspension bridges. One of the women shrieked something about the railway bridge that crossed the road by the pub.

The operator told her to wait, and she pushed herself up from the floor and took a seat close to the man. She felt a compunction to stay near him. Offer him company and protection, maybe.

On the floor by his lifeless hand was a slim paperback book, getting wet in the drizzle. Diana leaned over and picked it up. She turned it over in her hand; it was a copy of the mystery *At Bertram's Hotel* by Agatha Christie. A red

London bus on the cover, which made her smile despite herself.

A bookmark stuck out at an awkward angle. Diana opened the book to straighten it. The bookmark was a sheet of notepaper from the Redhouse Hotel.

Diana frowned.

She ran through the list of men signed up for the bridges tour in her head. If this man was staying at the Redhouse then the chances were he was one of theirs. But she couldn't place him.

The paper had a note, in blue biro. *Check the Pale Horse.* Beneath it, *Cat at Tower not in diary.*

She turned it over. *Pale Horse* was familiar, but she wasn't sure where from. But *Cat at Tower?* That meant nothing.

This man wouldn't be writing anything ever again. The fact that his final note was such nonsense made her sad.

"You shouldn't touch things."

She looked up to see Newton Crombie behind her. He peered past her at the dead man.

"It's just a book," she said, but she placed it on the seat across the aisle anyway.

"He's dead, is he?"

Newton stepped forward, wrinkling his nose as he gazed down at the man. Newton was the ultimate nerd, a man who was passionate about his hobbies and niche obsessions. Diana had never seen him get emotional, not even about his many children. Maybe about Gus the cat.

"He's dead," she said.

He tutted, pointing at the chrome head bar on the back of a seat. "Blood."

He was right. There was a long smear of blood on the curved corner.

Diana pinched the bridge of her nose with her thumb and forefinger. "Zaf has this theory that he might have fallen onto the bus."

"From where?"

She shrugged. "Tower Bridge?"

Newton bent to take a photo of the chrome headrest with his phone.

"You said we shouldn't touch anything," she said.

"I'm not touching. I'm taking a photo. The rain might wash it away and the police will want to know."

As if in response to the word *police* there came the sound of approaching sirens.

"Hey, hey, no." Newton reached out to grab Gus, who had been prowling under the seats towards the body.

Gus miaowed in complaint and batted at Newton's hand.

"Stop it now, fella." Newton held the big ball of cat against his chest and opened his jacket to shelter Gus from the drizzle. Gus licked the back of Newton's hand then gave it a tiny experimental bite.

"I'm not food," Newton said. "Stop taste-testing me."

Blue lights reflected off the wet railway bridge. The sirens stopped as a police car pulled up alongside the bus.

"I'll go meet them." Newton turned towards the steps, Gus safely inside his jacket.

There was chatter downstairs, followed by footsteps. Two officers in yellow hi-vis jackets and bulky stab vests appeared on the upper deck. One was female, tall with pale blonde hair pulled back in a bun. The other was male and stocky.

"Good morning," said Diana.

The male officer went straight to the body, dropping to a crouch to check for signs of life.

"Is this how you found him?" asked his colleague.

"Exactly like this," said Diana.

"Do you know who he is?"

"He might be one of our tour party. We only picked them up a couple of hours ago and I don't know all of them yet. Or he might not be one of our group at all." She didn't want to launch into theories about people falling from bridges.

"There's blood on my seats," Newton called from the stairs. "I took a photo. I haven't checked if he's dented it."

"If he fell, maybe it was an accident," Diana suggested.

"Lucy, come take a look at this," said the male officer.

His colleague came forward. There wasn't much room to manoeuvre on the upper deck but Diana could see they were inspecting the collar of the man's jacket, and his jawline.

The police officers quietly conferred and the man stood to speak into his radio.

"What is it?" asked Diana.

"I need you to come downstairs with me," said the female officer, Lucy. "And you need to tell me where the rest of your tour party is right now."

Diana wanted to ask what they'd seen.

"Ligature marks on the neck indicate possible strangulation," the male officer said into his phone. "Looks like he's been attacked."

Chapter Seven

Acting almost entirely on autopilot, Zaf got the tour group settled around the tables and booths of the Globe Tavern and spoke to the bar staff about getting drinks for everyone.

"Can I borrow this?" He lifted a food order pad and pen from the bar. The barman nodded.

A head count was the first priority, but here in the pub, it wasn't exactly easy. People were moving around, some taking the opportunity to use the toilets, and there were other patrons in here as well.

At least the hen party in their pink T-shirts were easy to identify. Zaf went round, taking names and writing them on his pad.

Kayleigh, Natalie, Katlyn, Phoebe...

The bride-to-be, Arwen, was taking snaps of herself with her older friend, Lydia, whose accent was purest London: not Wales like the rest of the group.

In the next booth along, the mother of the bride sat

fanning herself with a beer mat while her other daughter Bethan sat opposite, stroking the cast on her arm.

"Everything OK here?" Zaf asked.

Bethan smiled. "Any activity takes it out of Mum."

"I just need a moment," Gaynor said.

Zaf fetched a glass of water from the bar. Bethan murmured a *thank you* while Gaynor gulped it down and gasped. The woman probably wasn't even Diana's age, but she looked much older.

"There are good days and bad days," she said. "I keep a close record so I remember the good days." She tapped her handbag. "And there *are* good days. I have Hodgkin Lymphoma."

Zaf smiled. He'd heard of Hodgkin Lymphoma but beyond understanding it was life-threatening, he didn't know much about it.

"Lost the hair due to treatment." Gaynor pointed at her head.

Zaf smiled. "That is a lovely wig, if I may say."

She leaned back and returned the smile. "Thank you."

"No, really. It's stylish. May I suggest it's got a bit of that... oh, who was it in Charlie's Angels on TV? Farah Fawcett."

"I will take that compliment and put it in the diary," said Gaynor.

"And it goes well with those earrings."

Gaynor touched her dangly earrings. "These are Bethan's."

Bethan was inspecting her phone. "Not mine, precisely. I work in costume jewellery."

"Nice," said Zaf. "Design?"

"Manufacture. But it's still an artistic process."

Bethan's phone trilled and her face lit up. She raised it and showed the screen to Zaf and Gaynor. Three strawberries had lined up on a virtual slot machine.

"Fifty quid!"

Gaynor sighed.

"It was my daily free spin, Mum. Totally free." Bethan smiled at Zaf. "Mum worries about me."

Gaynor fished a thick purple diary out of her handbag. "Our Bethan is an absolute gem... Zack, is it?"

"Zaf."

"Zaf. Right. I do worry. Bethan needs to find a *good* man. Like her sister."

Zaf caught the emphasis on *good* and found himself wondering who or what had broken Bethan's arm.

"A good man is hard to find," he said with a grin. "Trust me, I've looked." Anything to lighten the mood.

"Oh." Gaynor frowned. "Oh!" She blushed.

Zaf chuckled. Gaynor clearly didn't have much of a gaydar.

"I need to check we've not lost any stragglers," he said, waving his notepad.

Gaynor opened her diary and lifted her pen. "Farah Fawcett, was it?"

"It was."

As Gaynor put pen to paper, Zaf moved on to the bridge-loving contingent. Two of them – Stuart and the improbably named Bunty – were arguing over the wine selection.

Zaf introduced himself to a few other men and added their names to the list.

Craig, Farhan, Alfie...

"I didn't know there were this many bridge fans," he said.

The man called Craig laughed. "Not necessarily *fans*.

This is mostly a jolly organised by our leader."

"Leader?"

Craig pointed towards Tom, the cantilever expert.

Zaf smiled. "Oh. Leader, huh?"

Just as Zaf was wondering whether Gaynor's faulty gaydar had twigged Tom, the man himself turned toward Zaf. They locked eyes, Tom giving him an impish smile.

Confident and charming. Cute, too.

Zaf had to know the man's second name. He made across the bar to speak to him.

As he was moving across the bar, the door opened and Diana entered, followed by two people who Zaf immediately identified as police detectives. He recognised them both.

His stomach lurched. *The man on the bus...*

He hurried to Diana and gestured back at the guests.

"I've not told them," he whispered. "They don't know. Or at least no one's said anything."

Diana tilted her head towards the great hulking bear of a detective beside her. "Detective Chief Inspector Sugarbrook here is in charge. It's a murder investigation."

The two of them had met DCI Sugarbrook before. More than once. The first time, a woman had been stabbed during a tour of the Houses of Parliament. The second time they crossed paths, a theatre director had fallen to his death from the rigging above a West End stage. On both occasions, Diana had solved the mystery before Sugarbrook had. With a little help from Zaf.

Zaf felt a wave of nausea.

"Murder?" he whispered.

"Zaf, isn't it?" said DCI Sugarbrook. "Have you done a headcount?"

Zaf swallowed and nodded. He added a mark to the pad

for Tom and then, seeing the two Colin Firth lookalikes across the bar, added two marks for them. "Twenty-one in total."

"That's what we should have," said Diana.

"Then our corpse is a mystery man," Sugarbrook said to the female detective next to him.

"He fell onto the bus, didn't he?" Zaf asked.

Sugarbrook looked at him. "Fell?"

When the detective chief inspector frowned, he looked like one of those heads on Easter Island.

"From Tower Bridge?" Zaf suggested.

"DS Quigley..."

"Already writing it down," said the female detective.

"Right." Sugarbrook sniffed. "We need to get this lot processed and interviewed."

"We don't have room at the nick," said DS Quigley.

Diana shook her head. "I don't think you need to take my entire tour party to the police station."

Zaf glanced over towards Gaynor and Bethan, who were staring at them, along with the other hens.

"Some of them are medically vulnerable," he said.

The bridge fans had also noticed the arrival of the detectives.

"What's going on here?" asked Bunty. "Someone been a bit naughty, eh?"

Zaf rolled his eyes.

"Detective Sugarbrook," muttered Diana. "All of this tour group are staying at the same hotel on Chiltern Street. May I suggest we take them back there and you can question them in comfort?"

"Not a bad idea, Guv," said DS Quigley.

"Fine," grunted Sugarbrook. "We separate out staff and

tourists. Twenty-one, you say? We get three vans up here."

"We can just go on the bus, can't we?" said Zaf.

"Sir," Quigley told him, "your bus is now a crime scene. It's going nowhere."

Zaf stared at her. Newton was not going to like this.

"We need to get it under cover for forensic examination," Sugarbrook explained. "Your depot's near the hotel, isn't it, Miss Bakewell?"

"It is."

He nodded. "Get Forensics to meet us at Chartwell and Crouch," he said to his sergeant, then turned to Diana, "Your driver happy to drive it back to the depot for us?"

"I think he'd rather it was him doing it than anyone else," she said.

Sugarbrook grunted and nodded.

"Is there a problem, officer?" called one of the hen party.

"Maybe it's the stripper!" said another, followed by laughter from the women.

"You've not told them anything?" Sugarbrook asked Zaf.

"Not a word."

Sugarbrook sighed. "Right." He turned to the room. "Listen up, ladies and gents! I need the attention of everyone who was on that bus outside. I'm Detective Chief Inspector Clint Sugarbrook. There has been an incident on the bus. A man has died."

He paused, watching faces for a reaction, then went on.

"I will need all of you to come with me and my officers. In a minute, I'm going to ask you to accompany me to the police vehicles outside—"

"Does this mean we're not going to Tower Bridge?" demanded Stuart, standing by the bar.

"Probably not today," said Zaf.

Chapter Eight

Diana had been wrong to worry that returning to the hotel in the back of a police van would upset the hen party. They piled in, delighted. One of them (who'd clearly managed a drink or two during their brief stop at the Globe Tavern) kept asking the driver if they could put the sirens and lights on.

Zaf was travelling in another of the vans, while a few of the guests were unsupervised in a third van. Diana knew these people spent almost their entire lives without direct supervision from a professional tour guide, yet there was something in the very fibres of her being that hated leaving her wards unattended.

The journey from Borough Market to Marylebone took them over Blackfriars Bridge. Diana hoped the bridge fans noticed it, although she wasn't sure the view from the back of a police van matched what they would have seen from the top deck of the bus.

As they drove, she mulled over how she was going to break the news to the Chartwell and Crouch manager. Paul

Kensington was a man who never took bad news well, and refused to acknowledge that sometimes, things just didn't go to plan. Ironic really, given how often he harped on about his 'agile' management style.

Paul was away for the day, at some business seminar in Lambeth, so she wasn't surprised when her call went straight to voicemail. Probably for the best.

"Paul, it's Diana. Just to let you know that we've had to curtail the tour today. There's been an incident and the guests are all being returned to the Redhouse Hotel. I can fill you in later."

It was the blandest and least informative message she could have left. But at least he'd been told.

Next she phoned Penny Slipper, their guest liaison at the Redhouse Hotel.

"We're coming back to the hotel," Diana told her. "All of us."

"What's happened?"

"Well, some of them are a bit shaken. There was a death on the bus."

"Oh no! That's terrible. How?"

"It's not clear. The police want to interview everyone. It was either this or we'd all have ended up at the police station."

"No, that's perfectly understandable," Penny replied. "This has to be better for our guests."

Diana felt some of the tension leave her. She could always rely on Penny. "Is there somewhere in the hotel where the police can do their interviews? A function room or something?"

"Hmm. We've got a wedding party in today and another

one tomorrow, but we should be able to find some room. Leave it with me."

Fifteen minutes later, the vans pulled up outside the Redhouse Hotel on Chiltern Street. DCI Sugarbrook and DS Quigley were already there waiting for them.

Diana stood on the pavement, directing the party from the vans into the hotel. Sugarbrook looked up at the sky as rain started to fall again.

"Your driver is taking the bus to the depot," he said. "I want to separate staff and tourists. Staff back to the depot, tourists here. We'll work through them all as quickly as we can."

Diana looked past him to see Zaf holding Gaynor's arm, guiding her into the hotel. The mother of the bride looked unsteady.

"I will stay with the guests," Diana told the DCI.

He pursed his lips. "You do know who's in charge here, don't you, Miss Bakewell?"

Diana nodded. She popped up her umbrella against the fresh rain.

"A good leader knows how to make use of available resources."

There was dark rumble from within Sugarbrook's barrel chest. At last he gave her a gruff nod.

"You stay, then." He turned to DS Quigley. "Staff, guests. Separate them out. Get staff ID and then wait for Forensics at the depot."

In the reception foyer, six of the women had crowded together on a long couch. They still wore their bunny ears.

Penny Slipper beckoned Diana over. She eyed Diana, then Sugarbrook, over the top of her screen. "We're a bit busy over the next day or so. It's going to be tricky, if I'm honest."

"Penny is just checking to see what room we can use for the interviews," Diana told the DCI.

"There is no *we*, Miss Bakewell. This is a police matter and not your concern. If it can't be accommodated here, then it's down to the station with everyone."

"I'm not so sure that's a good idea," Diana said. "You've seen that one of our ladies has a broken arm and another is clearly unwell. Let's try and keep them comfortable, shall we?"

Penny hummed. "I said it would be tricky, not impossible. I might have to move you at some point, but you can have function room one for now. It's part of a booking for a big wedding but they won't need it right away. As long as you don't mess things up, it'll be fine for you to sit in there."

Sugarbrook leaned over. "If we're going to do this then I need two things. I need a holding area for everyone, and I need a private area where we can conduct the interviews."

Penny gave him an exasperated look. She peered back at her screen. "The interview room... that one can be pretty small, I guess?"

"Small as you like," said Sugarbrook. "A cupboard if needs be."

Diana caught a flicker on Penny's face and gave her a smile. "A cupboard?"

Penny shrugged. "Needs must." She picked up the phone. "Carmen, it's Penny. I'll need you to make space in the store cupboard on the first floor. We can relocate some of the contents to the executive floor. And put some chairs in the cupboard. Yes, chairs. Enough for the police to use it as an interview room. Yes, it isn't big, I know." She looked at the man-mountain that was DCI Sugarbrook. "Yes, Carmen, I guess they will have to cope."

Chapter Nine

Along with the two Colin Firths and Detective Sergeant Quigley, Zaf walked along Chiltern Street from the Redhouse Hotel to the bus depot.

As they walked, DS Quigley gestured at the lookalikes. "So what's your role?"

"They're lookalikes that joined the tour," Zaf told her.

"Claude made a mix up," said Fake Sideburns.

Real Sideburns eyed Zaf. "*Somebody* made a mix up."

"Who are you supposed to be?" Quigley asked. "I can see we've got Piers Morgan, but who are *you* meant to be?"

Fake Sideburns scowled.

"They're both meant to be Colin Firth," Zaf said.

"But I shifted to Hugh Grant," added Fake Sideburns. "I'm versatile."

Quigley wrinkled her nose.

"We were doing a Bridget Jones-themed tour," Zaf explained.

The DS nodded. "Hmm. I prefer *Notting Hill*."

Fake Sideburns dropped into his Hugh Grant voice. "Oh,

oh, I can do a few lines from Notting Hill, if... if... if you'd like."

Quigley gave him a look. "I'm good, thanks."

They arrived at the depot to find Newton there with two male police officers. He didn't look happy.

"They say the bus is a crime scene and it needs to be secured." Newton grabbed Gus, who'd been about to jump onto the open platform at the back of the Routemaster.

"Do we offer them a cup of tea?" Zaf asked him. "I mean, it's almost a rule that if someone's here to do a job, they're offered tea."

"Did someone say cup of tea?" said the Hugh Grant-a-like.

Zaf smiled. "Kitchen's this way."

Hugh was ahead of him. "I think I know my way around a kitchen." The man performed a headcount. "Tea for everyone?"

Quigley shook her head. "I'll get back to the hotel once I've got everyone's names."

"Colin Firth." Real Sideburns pointed to himself, then to his colleague. "That's Hugh Grant."

The DS sighed. "Real names."

"Isn't life just a succession of roles?" suggested Hugh Grant. The detective gave him a withering look and he blushed. "Sorry. Terry Rolls. Actor. I was Gareth Booncastle's stand-in and stunt double for two series of *Snoop!* I played Falstaff at the Marine Theatre in Lyme Regis."

"Names are fine," said the DS. "I don't need CVs." She took everyone's name, had a brief, muttered conversation with her uniformed colleagues taping off the area round the bus, and left the depot.

Newton turned to Zaf. "They don't really think the dead person dropped off Tower Bridge, do they?"

"I don't know what they think. It's all a bit of a blur to be honest, Newton. A body on our tour bus. It's horrible."

Newton shifted Gus in his arms to tickle the big moggy's tummy. "I'll tell you one thing, Tower Bridge is not an obvious choice for someone to jump or fall off."

"No?"

"The walkway across is completely enclosed. There's access for staff to get out, but it's all locked up."

"You some sort of expert on Tower Bridge?".

Newton gave a small smile. "Let me show you something. It's not something I would normally share, but it might be relevant."

Zaf shuddered. "Lead the way."

Newton walked to the corner of the huge vehicle shed where he kept his tools. There was an engine inspection pit in the floor, so Zaf tended to avoid the area for fear of falling in. He skirted it nervously, glancing down.

Newton put Gus on the floor and picked up a metal rod with a plastic fixture on the end.

"This way." He opened a side door to reveal a service corridor running between the depot and the building next door. He raised his metal rod to the ceiling, finding the point where it fit into a slot. A quick twist, and a door was gently lowered.

"I never knew that was there," Zaf said.

Newton raised an eyebrow. "And why would you?"

An ancient but well-maintained metal ladder slid down. Newton grabbed Gus in his left hand then climbed up. At the top, he pulled on a light cord. "Come on up."

Zaf followed the bus driver up to find a sizeable loft

space, extending away across the top of the garage. The floor matched the contours of the ceiling below.

"You've got a secret lair," he said. "I can't believe it."

"It's always been here."

Zaf peered through the hidden space. How could something like this exist in central London without anyone monetising it? An unscrupulous property developer could make four apartments from this.

"Come over here." Newton beckoned him towards a set of interlinked tables and pressed a button on the side. Zaf approached to see a board joining all the tables together, and a little bus driving along a groove that ran along its length.

He grinned. "You've got your own train set up here. Well, *bus* set."

"Do you recognise it?"

"The bus?"

"The route."

Zaf looked closer. Newton had painted in roads as well as buildings. It was a work in progress, but clearly a passion project.

Newton looked at Zaf. "It's the 139 bus route from Golders Green to Waterloo."

"Oh." That meant little to Zaf. "It's very... attractive."

It was indeed attractive, verging on beautiful. It was a part of the world Zaf knew, rendered in miniature. A fragment of his London, condensed into an almost understandable form. There was a toyshop charm to it.

"Why are you showing me this?" he asked.

"This was the start of my plan to build a scale model of the entirety of central London."

"That *is* a project and a half."

"I've worked out that if I want to do all of London

between Chelsea and Rotherhithe, I'm going to need a space at least fifty metres across.

Zaf marvelled at the ambition. Months before, Paul Kensington had tried to redirect some of the Chartwell and Crouch tours to an unpronounceable travesty called the Londiniumarium which, like this, was a condensed version of the entire city into a single space. The key difference between this and the Londiniumarium was that Newton's work was a labour of pure love, a homage to a city he clearly adored.

"I've been working on a model of the London Eye over here," Newton said, "but this is what I want you to see."

He flicked another switch and a light came on over another table. A perfect scale model of Tower Bridge sat at its centre.

Zaf felt his jaw fall open. "Holy Moly, Newton, did you make this?"

"I did. It's scratch-built, HO scale."

"Not sure what that means... but wow."

"Scratch-built means it's not from a kit and HO scale means it's an eighty-seventh the size of the real thing."

Zaf wanted to touch it, to prove that it was real. He reached out and tapped a fingernail on one of the towers. It was perfect in every detail. The stone of the towers had the same biscuity look of the real ones and the ironwork was painted in the correct shades of blue and white. The whole thing was set on a base board that was textured and painted to look like the river.

"What's it made from?"

"All sorts," Newton replied. "Quite a bit of it is wood, but you can see here a dredger on the river based on a repurposed sardine tin. Gus helped with that part, obviously. I did have to 3D print some of the bridge's moving parts."

"Moving parts? You're joking me! Are you saying the bridge will open and close?"

"Of course." Newton pulled a face. "Want me to show you?"

Zaf nodded. He felt like an eager child.

Newton pressed a button and there was a whirring sound. Gus jumped up to watch. Zaf wondered how many times the cat had seen this in action.

"The arms! They're really coming up!" Zaf squealed.

"They are called bascules," Newton told him.

Zaf reached out to brush the road surface of the bascule. "It even *feels* like tarmac."

"I have a secret method for creating the texture." Newton tapped the side of his nose. "Textured paint on sandpaper."

"Amazing."

"Anyway, the point that I was trying to make was that the walkway up at the top is entirely enclosed," said Newton, pointing. "Tourists can walk across the top but they can't get out. It wasn't always like that. It used to be a draughty cast iron walkway but nowadays it's all sealed up with glass to keep people safe, and a bit warmer too."

Zaf peered at the top of the bridge. There were two walkways, lined with something that looked like Perspex.

He grinned. "There are tiny people inside!"

"Of course there are. What kind of model maker would I be if I didn't add little people so you can see the scale?"

Zaf stood up. "We'd better go and tell the police it wasn't a body from the bridge."

Newton sniffed. "They're the police. They probably know that already."

Chapter Ten

Back at the Redhouse Hotel, Diana led the tour group up to the function room Penny had found for them. It was a beautiful airy space on the first floor, with a series of tall Victorian windows overlooking Chiltern Street. Mirrors on the far wall and stylish chandeliers brought extra light. There were plush carpets and comfy chairs, and excellent views over the street below.

She admired the vast curtains that complemented the Victorian architecture. A William Morris design, perhaps?

"Are we going to get some drinks in here?" asked a man.

"Penny said she would have tea and coffee sent up for us," Diana told him, although that probably wasn't the kind of drink he had in mind.

"What happens now?" asked Bunty.

Diana gave him her most reassuring smile. "I believe we'll all need to be interviewed by DCI Sugarbrook. *They're* in charge now."

The man nodded absently.

The tour guests were taking seats, dotting themselves

around the generous space. Carmen, the cleaner, was busy removing things from a nearby cupboard, which Diana imagined was to serve as the interview room.

Diana approached the hen party. Mother of the bride Gaynor was breathless after climbing the stairs.

"You alright, Mum?" her daughter Bethan asked.

"I'm fine. Stop fussing. But I'll tell you what's not right," Gaynor continued. "The idea of you being shut up in a small cupboard with a strange man. He could be anybody."

"He's a policeman," one of the bridge fans called across from another table.

"I don't care who he is. Safeguarding rules apply to everybody, don't they?"

"If anyone would like the services of a chaperone," Diana said, "then Chartwell and Crouch would be pleased to assist."

DCI Sugarbrook stood in the open doorway. "If any of our witnesses feel vulnerable, then they are entitled to an appropriate adult. But a 'chaperone' is not the same thing as a person who is too nosey for their own good."

Diana frowned. "Have I struck you as nosey?"

"Yes."

She reconsidered. "Have I ever struck you as *frivolously* nosey?"

"Well, I think it's a good idea," said Gaynor. "I for one would feel much more comfortable with Diana there."

There was a chorus of "Me too!"

"What we need is a drink or two while we wait," called the thirsty man again.

DCI Sugarbrook shook his head with exasperation and called over to Carmen. "Cleaning lady, I'm afraid I don't know your name. We're going to need an extra chair in the cupboard, please." He pointed a finger at Diana. "You're first."

Diana could see that Carmen was working hard to turn the storage cupboard into an interview room. It was a decent sized walk-in cupboard, but she still had to empty storage boxes and cleaning supplies to clear the floor space.

"Can my officers help with that?" Sugarbrook asked, glancing at his watch.

Carmen shook her head. "No."

Sugarbrook gave Diana a look which she returned with a smile. Carmen was proud of her work. She wouldn't want the police messing up her system.

At last the cupboard was cleared and Carmen permitted the police to step inside. Diana followed to find that the snug windowless room was actually quite cosy.

Its faded white walls lent a glow to the space, and the little room smelled of freshly washed linen.

Satisfied, she placed herself on one of the chairs. Clint Sugarbrook squeezed himself behind a tiny table Carmen had put in there.

"Your colleague, Zaf Williams, counted twenty-one people in the pub."

Diana nodded. "There were twelve women on our Bridget Jones tour and eight men on the bridges tour."

"Bridges?"

"It started out as a typo, but... well, we might do it deliberately in future. Two tours in one. The package included a long weekend stay in London, so they were already here last night."

"Twelve women, eight men."

"Yes," she replied. "It would be nice to buck the stereotype, a male Bridget Jones fan or a female bridge spotter. But life isn't always like that."

"Twelve plus eight is twenty, not twenty-one," said Sugarbrook.

"I assume Zaf counted himself."

"Twenty guests. Zaf, you, the driver and then, out of nowhere, this body on the upper deck."

"Could anyone have sneaked on during the morning?"

"An old Routemaster bus has a limited number of entrances. Effectively, the only way on is via the open platform at the back. No, no one got on while the bus was in transit."

"Unless someone dropped onto the top..."

"Perhaps."

"The Colin Firth lookalike was also on the list..." Diana put her hand to her mouth. "No. There were two of them. Zaf should have counted twenty-two."

"Really?"

She nodded. "So that means..."

"It means our victim is someone who should have been on your bus. I'll need a list of names."

"I'll arrange it." She swallowed. How could she have missed that?

Sugarbrook eyed her. "Tell me how you found the body."

Diana recounted how she had gone upstairs to sweep the top deck for stragglers and had found the man on the floor.

"And you didn't recognise him?"

"No," said Diana. "We had only picked up the group two hours earlier and then they were straight onto the bus. I have a gift for recalling names and faces, but I don't have a photographic memory. And this poor man was lying face down."

"So he could be one of the tour party and your second lookalike led your colleague to confuse the numbers."

Diana frowned. "Possibly."

DCI Sugarbrook shook his head.

The door opened and Detective Sergeant Quigley entered. She regarded the space.

"This is small."

"Compact and bijou," suggested Diana.

Sugarbrook looked at the DS, a question on his face.

"Uniform are at the depot with the bus and the staff," she told him. "Waiting on Forensics. The body's on the way to the mortuary."

"He's been taken away already?" Diana said. "I thought the crime scene—"

"We weren't going to drive a body around on an open top bus, were we?" said Sugarbrook. He pointed at the room beyond the cupboard. "We need names and ID from all of those outside. We'll get someone to do photographs. We'll bring them in one at a time as soon as possible."

As the sergeant left, Sugarbrook looked at Diana once more.

"Was there anything in particular you noted about the body?"

"I didn't notice that he'd been strangled," she said. "I suppose I thought he might have just fallen and banged his head. There was blood on one of the headrest bars, Newton took a photo of it."

"The driver took photos of the crime scene?"

"I think he was worried the blood would wash away in the rain. Actually, I think he was also worried that the poor man had dented the metalwork on his bus. Oh, and there was the book."

"The book?"

"A detective novel. It was on the floor. I assumed it belonged to the man. The paper he was using as a bookmark was stationery from this hotel, which led me to assume he was one of our party."

"You picked up evidence from a crime scene?"

She met his gaze. "I picked up a book that was getting wet in the rain, Detective."

"And now your fingerprints are on it."

"Is an Agatha Christie novel likely to be key evidence in this crime?"

"You never know," said Sugarbrook. "You never know."

DS Quigley pushed open the door, and gave Sugarbrook an anxious look.

"Nineteen, Sir. There are only nineteen people out there."

Sugarbrook's face twisted in annoyance. "Lord preserve us from people who can't count."

Chapter Eleven

Diana placed her phone on the table between herself and DCI Sugarbrook. She had Zaf on speakerphone.

"Zaf," she said, "We need to check. You said there were twenty-one people in the pub."

"That's right," replied Zaf.

"Including you?"

"No. Was I meant to count myself?"

"Twenty-one people, including yourself and the two lookalikes? We had twenty booked on the tour."

"Oh," said Zaf on the phone. "The lookalikes. They're here now. But we only had one on the list."

Diana glanced between the two detectives, then back at her phone. "The Colin Firths are at the depot?"

Quigley frowned. "You asked us to split up tourists and staff, Sir. They said they were staff."

Sugarbrook sighed. "Then we need to talk to them too." He leaned back, hitting his head on a shelf of cleaning supplies. "So we *are* missing a member of the tour party."

"I don't think anyone actually fell onto the bus," said Zaf.

"No," said Diana. She picked up her phone, careful not to lose the call, and scrolled through her emails to find the list of tour guests. As she did so, she noticed that a voicemail had come through from Paul Kensington. That could wait.

Quigley checked her notepad. "ID in the man's pocket names him as David Medawar."

Diana nodded. "One of our passengers. I'm sorry I didn't recognise him earlier."

Sugarbrook made a sucking sound.

"Thanks, Zaf," said Diana. "We'll speak later." She ended the call.

"A body with a name," said Sugarbrook. "A man who died on the bus. We will want to interview these two lookalikes pronto."

"They definitely didn't go upstairs," Diana told him. "There was a lot of moving around, particularly after most of the men came downstairs to get out of the rain. But the two actors never went upstairs. They were on the phone to their agent and then they were busy with selfies until we got to the Globe. It was quite chaotic but I can assure you, they never went upstairs."

"Chaotic, hmmm?" Sugarbrook said. "Right, we'd best get on with the initial interviews. Since it's a hen party, we'll start with the bride-to-be, shall we? Little Miss Chaperone, you can stay here if you wish but I'll not be having a word out of you."

Diana raised an eyebrow at his tone, but nodded her agreement.

After a few moments, which Sugarbrook spent immersed in his phone, Arwen squeezed in next to Diana. She had a grin on her face and a bouncy energy.

"Are you OK?" asked Sugarbrook.

"Oh, I'm fine. It's all just a bit exciting." Arwen tapped Diana's arm. "If this turns out to be one of those immersive murder mystery things and it's all just put on for me, I'll be giving you five stars."

"It's not an immersive murder mystery thing," Sugarbrook grunted.

"I mean, it's obviously a deviation from the Bridget Jones tour but that was always Mum's thing, not mine."

"This is very real, Miss Griffiths. Soon to be Mrs...?"

"Oh, I am keeping my surname when I get married. Keagan's a lovely guy but I live in London now and I'm not giving up my professional name." She puffed out her chest. "I'm an influencer and a social media statement marketer."

Sugarbrook cocked his head. Was that a smile flickering at his lips?

"So," he said, "you live in London but the rest of your group came from your home town in Wales."

"Merthyr Tydfil. Mum and Bethan are from there, Phoebe and Natalie too. But not Lydia. She's London like me. We work closely together. We have this social media narrative. It's very cute. We both live in Wembley. Do you know it?"

"Do I know Wembley?" said Sugarbrook. "Yes, Arwen, I do. Do you know a man called David Medawar?"

Arwen frowned then shook her head.

"I don't think so. I do meet a lot of people, though."

DS Quigley showed her a picture on his phone.

From where she was sitting, Diana could see this wasn't a picture of a corpse. It was a thin-faced man with tanned features, wearing a pale polo shirt in bright sunlight. A holiday snap, she guessed, shared on Facebook or Instagram.

"I don't know him," Arwen said. "Is that the dead man?"

Sugarbrook nodded. "We think he was garrotted on the bus, while you were on it."

Arwen stared at him.

"Do you know what garrotted means, Arwen?" asked Sugarbrook.

Arwen shook her head.

"It means he was strangled using an item, like a rope, or a cord or a belt."

"Oh!"

"Someone wrapped something around his neck and then pulled and squeezed with all their might until he was dead."

"That's terrible," said Arwen, the humour and excitement now drained from her face.

"Yes, it is," said Sugarbrook. "David was from Brazil originally, but lived in London. You're the only other member of the party from London. So can you take a look at the photograph again and tell me if you recognise him at all?"

Chapter Twelve

The Forensics unit had now arrived at the Chartwell and Crouch depot, a team of three in a single van who quickly set up a table of equipment outside the bus and climbed into white protective suits that included overshoes and masks.

Zaf offered them all a drink. Brewing pots of tea for police officers and crime scene investigators was hardly part of his job description, but he wanted to be helpful.

He was aware that people didn't always take him seriously, especially online, where he knew his presence could be shallow. Sometimes he'd go days and realise that all he'd posted was the latest miracle moisturiser he'd found in the shops.

He was intrigued by the fact that Diana had kept a diary as a younger woman. He wondered if it was anything like *Bridget Jones' Diary*, all cigarettes, alcohol and hot men. Maybe Zaf needed a diary or a journal to help him become the serious and respected man he wanted to be.

He took a tray of mugs and placed them on the edge of

the CSI team's table. As one of the three came out to grab one, Zaf saw Gus the cat sauntering onto the bus. Had they noticed him? Surely his presence wouldn't be helpful.

He sat down with Newton on one of the chairs Newton had put out to observe.

"I hope they're not using any corrosive or staining agents on my bus," Newton said.

Zaf sipped his tea. "I'm sure it'll be fine."

"I mentioned the blood mark on the head rest upstairs. The bloke said it was probably a post-mortem injury."

"Hmmm?"

"The man fell forward and banged his head after he was already dead."

"Do people bleed when they're dead?"

Newton shrugged.

Zaf watched through the windows of the bus as the three white-suited people moved around. "I did hear a thump from upstairs when we were going across Tower Bridge."

"The dead man falling out of his seat," Newton said. "By the way, I just saw Gus get on the bus."

"I know. I was going to say something but I'm sure they'll work it out for themselves," replied Zaf.

A moment later, a technician appeared at the door of the bus with Gus cradled in her arms. She gently dropped him to the floor. Another technician began taking pictures of the bus.

"Uh oh, a camera," said Newton.

Zaf knew what he meant.

Newton raised an eyebrow. "Gus loves to be in photos."

"There's a name for people who enjoy being in the limelight as much as Gus."

"I don't think you can apply the same judgements to cats, Zaf."

Zaf saw Gus trotting over, his tail held high. He sat and posed each time the technician aimed his camera.

"Maybe they won't notice," said Zaf.

Every photo the technicians took, there was Gus. The door to the bus (with added Gus): click. The stairs to the upper deck (with added Gus): click. The upper deck itself (with yet more Gus): click.

Zaf could hear small grunts of frustration.

"I've got an idea," he called over. "Gus will soon notice if someone else is taking photos." He glanced at Newton. "Come on, then."

Newton shuffled in his seat. "What?"

Zaf pulled out his phone. "We're doing a photoshoot of our own. Come on, Newton, smile for the camera!"

Newton gave a smile that looked like it had been painted on by someone who'd never seen a real smile. A few moments later, there was a blur in Zaf's peripheral vision and Gus was sitting on the back of Newton's chair, gazing into the lens.

Newton's smile grew genuine and Zaf took more pictures. He kept going, getting pictures of Gus on Newton's lap, Gus being held in the air in the style of *The Lion King*, Gus taking a selfie with his own paw (which was harder than Zaf expected).

He looked over to see that the CSIs had finished taking their photos.

"I think we might be done with the photoshoot now, Gus. Well done." He gave Gus a ruffle between the ears. "You are such a handsome chap."

Chapter Thirteen

Diana listened, trying not to draw attention to herself, as Gaynor Griffiths, the mother of the bride, gave her statement. She spoke slowly, with consideration: almost as if she were expecting a certificate for getting it right.

"I do not recall seeing that man," she said.

"You didn't go upstairs on the bus at any point during the tour that morning?" asked DCI Sugarbrook.

"I was too busy having fun with my girls. Besides, me and stairs do not get on well."

"You've been unwell recently, yes?"

Gaynor nodded. "Hodgkin Lymphoma."

"I'm not familiar with it."

"It's a cancer of the lymph system. Little lymphocytes start reproducing out of control. I had this huge swelling under my arm. The hospital put me through courses of chemotherapy and radiotherapy which –" She laughed. "Let me tell you, that takes it out of you even months after they've stopped."

"I see. Well, we will make sure you're as comfortable as possible out there. I think refreshments will be brought up at some point."

"I never go anywhere without drinks and snacks." Gaynor put her considerable handbag on the table. "A girl's got to keep her strength up." She delved into her bag. "Wafer biscuits, mini-cookies, my big bottle of vitamin smoothie."

Diana saw a look pass between Sugarbrook and DS Quigley.

"Mrs Griffiths," said the DCI, "the dead man was strangled with a rope or cord or similar. That handbag of yours has a nice long strap."

Gaynor's eyes widened. "I said I was downstairs the whole time."

"We will need to take that away for examination."

"But it's my *bag*."

"We will find you another one in the meantime."

"Let me have a look," said Diana.

She stepped out of the cupboard interview room. The function room outside was a good size, and the two groups had gravitated to different areas. The bridge group sat in sombre silence, looking out at the rain that pattered noisily on the windows. The thrill of being taken away by the police was wearing off.

The hen party, in contrast, seemed to be exploring ways to entertain themselves. Arwen still had her huge woven bag, and had pulled out giant glittery sunglasses for everyone. They posed for pictures, smiling at each other.

Diana went to the door where two uniformed officers stood.

"No one is to leave the room, Madam," said one.

"We're not prisoners here," she told him. "We're helping

the police with their enquiries. Why do people always use those words? It really does sound like the police are struggling, like it's a maths test and they need help. Listen, I need to go find a bag for Gaynor to—"

She was interrupted by the doors opening.

"Coffees and teas as promised," said Penny, wheeling a trolley into the room. "I'll see if I can grab a few little snacks as well. It's getting late and you must be starving."

Through the open door there came the distant sound of music. The wedding in the other part of the hotel.

The mood in the room lifted at the sight of the trolley, and there was a general movement towards it.

"I was telling these officers I need a carrier bag or something similar," said Diana.

Penny gave her a smile then reached below the trolley and whipped out a white carrier bag marked with a coffee company logo.

"That will do perfectly." Diana returned to the interview room.

Gaynor was taking the contents of her handbag and dumping them on the table so she could give it to the police.

"We can do that," said Sugarbrook.

Gaynor eyed him. "I'll be doing it, thank you."

Diana helped the woman transfer her possessions to the carrier bag. There was a purse, keys, a thick day-per-view diary and a rather attractive metallic pen. Diana put keys, receipts and other scrappy items in the carrier bag.

"I'll hold onto that," said Gaynor, retrieving a chunky flip-top drinking bottle full of a fruity sludge. She noticed Diana looking at it.

"Raspberry and banana," she said. "I'm sure it's full of sugar really but I've got to get those vitamins. I had to make them for myself for a week or two and I swear they gave me the energy to push on through."

"Thank you for this," said Sugarbrook and put the handbag aside. "We will return it as soon as we've examined it."

"I told you I didn't kill Mr Medawar."

"We leave no stone unturned," he said. "I'll let you take a break. Did I hear there was tea and coffee outside?"

Diana carried Gaynor's carrier bag for her as they returned to the function room.

Penny's *little snacks* were much more impressive than the words implied. Little vol-au-vents and fish things on crackers had been set out on the tables in the room, together with tiny pastry parcels of mystery. The two tour groups dug in hungrily.

A man in a silk shirt approached Diana. "How much longer is this going to take?"

She gave him a smile, recalling that his name was Tom and he had extensive knowledge of bridge construction.

"Who are you?" said Sugarbrook from the cupboard doorway.

"Tom Hatcher. Founder and owner of Bifrost solutions."

"We'll talk to you next then," said Sugarbrook. "You don't need a chaperone, do you?"

He looked at Diana, his eyes twinkling. "Oh, absolutely." He took her arm and steered her back to the cupboard.

As they walked, he leaned in close. "I overheard what you did," he whispered. "Thank you for arranging to keep us here rather than the police station. My friends and investors might cease to be one or the other or even both if we'd been carted off to the nick."

Diana shrugged. "Least I could do. What's Bifrost?"

"My company. At its core is some revolutionary technology to build bridges in adverse conditions."

"That sounds very useful."

"Like all great innovations, it's actually a ridiculously simple idea. Imagine if you will a crossbow—"

"Mr Hatcher," said Sugarbrook, with a cough, gesturing into the cupboard room.

"Of course." Tom took a seat.

Diana took the seat next to him and DS Quigley closed the door.

"Tom Hatcher," said Sugarbrook, looking at his notes.

"That's me." Tom smiled.

"Seems you're the lynch-pin of the little bridge tour."

"Am I?"

"Half the fellers out there say they're only here because this is a little jolly you've put on for the investors in your company."

Tom nodded. "Sort of an early investor reward. I'm an engineer. Bridges are my thing. I've got a business meeting with Tower Division Engineering later tomorrow. We're going to go into full production on my revolutionary design."

"Yes, yes, very nice. David Medawar was one of your investors, wasn't he?"

Tom's smile dropped.

"Yes." He licked his lips. "Yes, he was. He's your corpse, isn't he?"

"He is," said Sugarbrook. "If you don't mind me saying, you don't seem particularly cut up about it."

"I..." Tom paused. "I'm not. Emotionally. That might seem callous. Probably not a good idea when you're looking for a killer. But people die every day. Gosh, that *does* sound callous. I knew him as an investor, not as a friend."

"And yet most people would be upset to discover someone they knew, even 'just' as an investor, had been murdered."

"If it's any help, my mother had me tested for Asperger's," said Tom. "I can pretend to be emotional if you wish. I like to think I'm a gifted actor and liar." He took a beath. "Again, not a wise thing to say when talking to the police. You'd prefer me to be honest, right?"

"I would," said Sugarbrook.

"Good. I knew David online. He was less interested in the design work of Bifrost and more interested in it as a business opportunity. I don't think he looked up at a single bridge this morning. Had his face buried in a book."

"What book?"

"*At Bertram's Hotel*," said Diana. "Sorry. Didn't mean to butt in."

"The Agatha Christie," said Sugarbrook.

"I suppose you think detective novels are silly," said Tom. "As a police detective."

Sugarbrook nodded. "The motives are too clean and the murderers are always too competent for my liking."

"Too competent?"

"Nine times out of ten, murders are committed by foolish and reckless people who act out of desperation. They rarely plot or plan. And again, nine times out of ten, the murderer is not someone with an obscure reason to kill the victim. It's the parent or the spouse or the best friend."

"None of us on the bus were that to David," Tom said. "Unless I'm mistaken, none of us had even met him before last night at the hotel."

"And yet one of the tour group killed David a few hours ago."

Tom frowned. "It is, indeed, a mystery."

Sugarbrook consulted his notes. "David Medawar lived in London. Why would he stay at the hotel if he lived locally?"

Tom grinned. "Don't you take the opportunity to stay in an upscale hotel whenever it's offered?"

"I think my other half might have words if I stayed away for a night without good reason."

"David didn't have a partner. No family in the area. Or the country, I believe. British-Brazilian if I recall correctly. His elderly parents are still over there. Maybe that's why he chose to stay at the hotel. When I got in last night I saw him enjoying a drink with a couple of the women."

"The women?" asked Sugarbrook.

Tom jerked his head back to indicate the function room behind. "The older woman and her daughter. You know, the one with the broken arm."

Diana glanced towards the door.

Gaynor had denied ever meeting David Medawar. Yet Tom was saying she'd had drinks with him the night before.

Diana opened her mouth to speak, but was stopped by Sugarbrook's stare.

Sugarbrook shifted his gaze onto Tom. "I see." He made a note in his pad.

Chapter Fourteen

Zaf and Newton sipped tea as the Forensics team continued with their work. They'd put down yellow markers to mark significant spots, mostly on the upper deck. Zaf couldn't see them all from where he was, but he could hardly avoid noticing as one of them came sailing through the air and landed by his feet.

He looked up and saw Gus peering over the top deck rail, looking pleased with himself.

He chuckled. "Gus'll get us all thrown in jail."

Gus disappeared for a moment then reappeared with another yellow marker in his mouth. He dropped it over the side of the bus.

"Oi!"

One of the white-suited technicians appeared over the top of the bus, glaring down at the marker on the ground. Gus ran off.

"I'm so sorry!" Zaf called. "He's very playful and he wants to be involved. I'm pretty sure he's trying to help."

"This is a crime scene."

"Look, I've got an idea. Have you got spares?"

"Spare markers? Sure."

"Let me borrow some of them and I'll distract him. And... we might need to do the same for any other equipment you're using."

The technician gave Zaf a look. "Seriously? You're going to set up a fake crime scene to entertain the cat? Can't you just lock him in a cupboard or something?"

Newton leaned forward in his chair. "We are absolutely going to entertain the cat rather than lock him in a cupboard. We are not monsters."

The technician held up his hands, and then went to fetch Zaf and Newton some supplies. "Here. Just keep this well away from the actual crime scene. Here is some tape and some markers. You'll need some of this fingerprint dusting powder and the brushes to apply it."

Zaf exchanged glances with Newton. "Really?"

"If you're going to fake a crime scene to entertain a cat," the technician said, "you might as well do it properly. Here are some evidence bags and tweezers. Make sure to mark the bags as 'fake evidence' or something, yeah?"

Zaf nodded turned to Newton, grinning. "Come on then, let's go do some crime scene work."

"Shall we put on boiler suits," Newton asked, "so that we look the part?"

"Really?"

"How often will you get a chance to dress up like a proper SOCO?"

"SOCO?"

"Scenes of Crime Officer."

"Oh, OK. Well, we might need to pull out all of the stops if we want Gus to find us as interesting as the professionals."

Newton found two boiler suits in a maintenance cupboard. "Where shall we set up our crime scene?"

"What about Paul Kensington's office?" Zaf suggested. "I think he's still out for the day. It's a confined space, so we can make sure Gus doesn't get distracted."

They stretched crime scene tape across the door of the office and called for Gus, who appeared while they were putting out the yellow plastic markers.

"Where do these go?" asked Newton.

Zaf shrugged. "It doesn't matter, it's all pretend."

Newton nodded towards Gus. "Shhh! He can hear you. He's a smart cat and he can detect fakery." He scanned the floor of Paul's office. "Tell you what, I'll mark the outline of a body, so we can visualise what we're doing. Pass me Paul's tape dispenser."

Chapter Fifteen

Bethan shuffled on her seat in the interview cupboard, giving Sugarbrook a wary look then resting her arm in its cast on the tiny table. DS Quigley was holding out a phone with a Facebook photo displayed.

"I am sorry," she said. "My mum, she gets very tired. And that makes her forgetful. Yes, I do know that man. David, right?"

"Correct," said DCI Sugarbrook as DS Quigley pocketed the phone. "You met him last night. You seem to be one of very few people here who spoke to him. Or *remembers* speaking to him."

"Oh, that's nice," she said. "I mean, it's nice that I can be helpful."

Sugarbrook leaned back. The chair creaked alarmingly at his shifting bulk. "Tell us about David Medawar."

Bethan's eyes widened. She looked down at her cast, thinking.

"We'd come into the hotel restaurant cos we'd just

arrived from Paddington Station and we were absolutely famished. Well, I was. Mum's appetite comes and goes. And there wasn't really anywhere to sit but the waitress asked this man if he'd mind sharing his table. That was David. You want me to describe him? He was, like, tall and going thin on top a bit but not in an unattractive way—"

"We know what he looked like, Miss Griffiths," said Sugarbrook. "What was he like as a person? What did you talk about?"

Bethan nodded. "He asked me about my arm." She lifted her arm in its cast. "It's quite the conversation starter. I told Arwen I was thinking of keeping it until the wedding, draw a few eyes, but she told me that no bridesmaid of hers was going to be in her wedding photos with a cast on her arm."

"Arwen is your younger sister?"

"She is."

"I think everyone here has seen that you care for your mother a lot."

"I do. I suppose caring isn't Arwen's strong suit, really. I mean I love her, I do, but she's got a lot of... self-focus. You seen her Instagram and TikTok? Oh! It's like twenty-four-seven, six days a week."

"You pick up a lot of the strain," said Sugarbrook. "You were telling us about David Medawar."

"Right. So, I was. He opened the conversation, but not like he was trying anything on. Just friendly chit-chat like. He's got a job that's something in chemicals. Had a job, I guess."

Diana saw Bethan's face sag with sadness for a moment, and realised it was the first sign of real emotion anyone had shown.

"He seemed really nice," Bethan said. "I mean, kind of

boring, but nice, still. He talked about his job and it was all chemical plants this and polymers that. I don't think I understood but I didn't really care. You don't have to be interested in what a man does to like him, do you? They're all nerds at heart, aren't they?"

Diana thought of Newton Crombie, wondering briefly what he and his wife talked about in the evenings. Probably all those children.

"Did you like him?" asked Sugarbrook.

Bethan laughed, making her earrings swing.

"I'd only just met him, hadn't I? What do you think I am? And I was with my mum. You know, having your mum with you isn't... what's the word? It's not good for picking up men. Conducive! It's not conducive. No, we just chatted."

"What about? Did you chat about polymers and chemicals all evening?"

Bethan sighed. "No. I don't know. The usual stuff. The factory I work at, he was interested in that. I do stocktaking, so it's all double-Dutch to me. And then somehow Mum got the conversation turned round so she could talk about her illness. That's her hobby. She can bore for Wales, like Olympic standard, on the subject of Hodgkin Lymphoma. She was telling him everything about it, the hospital visits, the biopsy, the treatment. He listened politely enough but he wasn't interested."

"Did he mention anyone else while you were talking? Did he mention this tour or anyone on it?"

Bethan nodded. "Oh, we did have a laugh when we realised we were on the same tour. Bridget Jones and bridges. I don't know who came up with that one. Sounds like someone made a cock-up, I reckon. Yes, he was meeting these bridge people for the first time. I don't know how many of them knew each other in real life. I got the impression that he didn't really want to be here."

"He *didn't* want to be here?"

"No, not at all. But it was work. That hi-tech bridge project they'd all invested in."

"I thought this was just a little free thank-you trip for investors," said Sugarbrook, glancing at Diana.

Diana gave a polite shrug. "We just sell the tickets and do the tour."

"It was definitely work for him," said Bethan, "He had a thing to sort out."

"What thing?"

"I don't know, but it was definitely a thing." She waved her good hand. "A difficult conversation."

"What was?"

"No, he said he was going to have to have a difficult conversation."

"Who with?"

Bethan shrugged. "I don't know. But that was why he was here."

"Thank you," said Sugarbrook. "And, if you don't mind me asking, what did happen to your arm?"

Bethan looked down at her cast. "This is weeks old."

"Yes. But how did it happen?"

Bethan pulled back a little, her expression tight.

"Is it a painful subject?" asked Sugarbrook. "Excuse the pun."

"Depends what my mum's been telling you."

"Why? What would she say?"

Bethan pursed her lips. "I've not been so lucky with the fellers in recent years. Being a full-time carer and holding down a full-time job doesn't leave much time for anything else. I don't have no hobbies. When my day is done, I've only got time to play a few games on my phone and then I'm zonked out."

"Unlucky with the fellers," Sugarbrook prompted.

"Daryl was never right for me. I mean he was lush but he'd never really got over his last divorce and, I admit, he was too fond of a drink."

Sugarbrook indicated the cast. "He did that to you?"

"No!" replied Bethan. "No, he didn't. But trying to get my mum to believe that... *This* I did by walking into a lamppost at night, looking left and right when I should have been looking ahead. Daft. But not if you talk to my mum. She thinks I've got atrocious taste in men and her little girl needs... Well, anyway, she doesn't believe my lamppost story."

"Should *we*?" said Sugarbrook.

"Pardon?"

"Should *we* believe your lamppost story?"

Bethan's face froze for a second. Then she laughed.

"Oh, my mum would love you! It was a lamppost, Mr Officer Sir. Honestly. Did it on a lamppost. Put me right out of action for the best part of a fortnight."

"And how is it now?" he asked.

"Nearly healed, I reckon."

"You can use your arm fully?"

"I reckon so."

"Do you mind taking hold of my hand?"

Sugarbrook's outstretched hand was a big meaty thing, and Bethan could only grip his top two fingers.

"Pull," he said. "As hard as you can."

"If you say so." She tugged, hard. His hand barely budged.

"Doesn't hurt?" he said.

"No." She let go.

"Sounds like that cast is ready to come off."

"But it's like I say, a bit of a conversation starter. And I like stirring it up with Arwen, making her think I'm gonna keep it on for the wedding."

"Thank you." Sugarbrook gestured to the door. Bethan stood, her arm less awkward now, and left.

Diana frowned at the DCI. "Do you think she realised you were testing whether she was strong enough to strangle a man?"

He blinked back at her. "Was *that* what I was doing?"

Chapter Sixteen

In the 'crime scene' in Paul Kensington's office, Newton got Zaf to lie on the floor so he could mark around his body with tape.

"This is good," said Newton. "Now we can put the yellow markers on the places where the bullets made entry wounds."

"Was I shot?" asked Zaf in horror. He pulled on a fake grimace. "Ouch."

Newton took pictures and moved around the room. Zaf tuned out his chat about bullet trajectories and blood spatter, instead watching Gus posing on the outline.

"We'll need to test for gunshot residue," said Newton.

"I don't think we've got that stuff. Only fingerprint powder."

"I'll go and ask."

Newton stepped over the tape at the door and returned a few minutes later.

"They said we're not wasting their swabs on the cat and

that we should use a cotton bud." He held up a cotton bud and crouched on the floor beside the outline.

"Don't they test people's hands with those?" Zaf asked. All he knew about this stuff was from his mum watching *Inspector Morse* reruns on TV.

Newton shrugged. "Maybe. Pass me the victim's hand, please."

Zaf rolled his eyes and knelt down by the outline. "Right or left?"

"We can do both, but you will need to label the baggies accordingly."

"Right." Zaf lifted an imaginary dead person's hand and turned it palm-up for Newton.

Newton wiped the cotton bud firmly across the imaginary palm and held it up. "Bag it and mark it."

Zaf looked at Newton. How had he ended up in the role of assistant?

Gus was transfixed, which was the main thing. The cat batted a plastic bag from the pile.

"See! He's helping!" cried Newton. "I knew it, he is the smartest cat."

Zaf eyed Gus. *Probably a coincidence.* He found a pen and labelled the bag.

Left hand GSR swab. FAKE EVIDENCE!!

He hoped that would satisfy the cat, who he was fairly sure couldn't read. Not to mention Newton, who was now impatient to do the other hand.

They repeated the process and Zaf bagged the evidence. Gus patted the bag in approval.

"Right," said Newton, "fingerprints next."

Zaf eyed the bus driver. Was he starting to believe they

were genuinely collecting evidence? He seemed even more absorbed than the cat.

Newton uncapped a small pot of powder and whisked a little brush in the top. He shook off the excess and twirled it up the legs of a nearby chair. "I wonder what this powder's made from. I hope it won't stain."

Zaf peered at the chair. "It looks fine to—"

"I mean the bus! People don't realise how much care a vintage vehicle needs to keep it looking as good as ours."

Zaf nodded. "Right. I'm sure it'll be fine. Can you see any fingerprints there?"

"Loads. Should we transfer them onto some tape or just take pictures of them?"

"I think just taking pictures should work fine."

Newton pulled out his phone and started to capture images of the ghostly imprints on the chair leg. Gus the cat stepped forward to take a look too, and Newton tickled him under the chin as he worked.

"We should test our own fingerprints so that we can rule ourselves out," said Newton. "And pawprints, obviously. Come here Gus, we can do you now."

"Rule ourselves out of what?" Zaf asked.

"Having touched this chair leg." Newton gave Zaf an *of course* look. "I'll need to get hold of the software to compare fingerprints, but that should be simple enough."

"Should it?" Zaf was no longer certain whether they were entertaining the cat, or Newton.

Gus sat perfectly still while Newton dabbed his paw onto one of the evidence bags, and dusted it with powder.

There was a grunted exclamation from the doorway. "What on earth is going on here?"

Zaf sprang up from the floor. "Paul! You're back, we thought you'd left for the day."

"Has... has something happened in here?" Paul Kensington approached the tape, aghast.

Zaf could imagine how it must look. There was the outline of a body, evidence bags scattered across the floor, and a suited technician examining a chair leg and a cat.

And Paul couldn't see Newton's face, so might think he was a genuine forensics officer. Not a bus driver playing with a cat.

There was a moment where Zaf could have explained that this was all being done simply to keep Gus away from the real crime scene, and that nothing in the office was real evidence. Instead he opted to keep his mouth shut, shrug his shoulders and pull a face as if he had no real idea.

A second later, he opened his mouth to speak, but by then it was too late. Paul Kensington made an annoyed huffing sound before turning on his heel and leaving the depot.

"He's gone!" Zaf whispered to Newton.

"Hmm?" said Newton, absorbed with Gus's pawprints. "Who's gone?"

Chapter Seventeen

Clint Sugarbrook looked at the paperwork and notes arrayed on the little table in the cupboard interview room and huffed.

"I think I might need a coffee break."

Diana nodded. "A good plan."

She stepped out of the cupboard and allowed the door to close behind her.

There was a clattering sound and a new voice rang out.

"Well this is fun!"

A man with a large camera bag had entered the room. The police at the door were speaking to him.

"I'm the photographer," he announced. He waved a hand at the assembled witnesses. "We need photos, don't we?"

"Right," said the police officer. "The guv wants individual shots of everyone."

"Of course." The photographer fingered the shoulder strap of the officer's stab vest. "This is a nice touch."

He moved around the room, grabbing pictures of people where they sat or stood.

Diana watched, puzzled. Wouldn't the police separate people out, take proper mugshots?

The photographer spent some time circling the women, most of whom were still wearing novelty sunglasses and bunny ears.

"Can I have a group shot?" he asked.

"Group shot?" Diana could see confusion on the faces of the uniformed officers by the door.

"You are looking so good, ladies!" said the photographer. "It's like Playboy bunnies went to see Elton John and got carried away at the merch stall."

The women gathered together and pouted at his lens as he directed them.

"Please tell me you have tails as well! No? Do we want to waggle imaginary tails? A cheeky little over-the-shoulder shot?"

The women posed with their hips swung out, looking over their shoulders. Arwen embraced Lydia, Gaynor was supported by Bethan, but everyone was smiling or laughing.

"Will we get copies of these?" asked Arwen.

"Sure you will!" said the photographer. "Now, let's take a look at the gents. What can we do here?"

He went over to the bridge group and gazed at them thoughtfully.

"I'm getting 'captain of industry' vibes from your faces. Serious, but proud and intense. Should we go with that? If I can get you to pose around this table, I think we can conjure a nice scene. Come on, over here. You've just brokered the deal of a lifetime, it's the making of you all, but you need your game faces on until the ink on that contract's dry. Chest out, chin up! Nice!"

He clicked at them as he ducked up and down, grabbing shots from every angle.

"Beautiful! What a great crowd you are, seriously."

Diana stared on, uncertain as to whether she should intervene. She wasn't entirely sure what was going on, but whatever it was, it would definitely be well-documented.

Sugarbrook emerged from the interview cupboard. "What is this?"

The photographer turned towards him and took a snap.

"You lot look just like the real deal," he said. "We all know Melanie loves a bit of drama, but this is next level stuff."

Sugarbrook approached the man, looming over him. "Melanie?"

"Can we use the handcuffs and the batons? Swing them a bit for me, will you? No? Not at all? You're more serious than that, I get you. Very much in role."

Sugarbrook looked at the officers by the door. "Who is this?"

"Photographer," said one.

The photographer moved around Sugarbrook. "Loving it. You are gritty northern drama cop-type police. You've seen it all. Nothing fazes you. We might need some lighting changes to properly capture the craggy contours of your—"

"Stop it now!" DCI Sugarbrook stepped forward, blocking the photographer with his physical bulk. "What on earth do you think you're doing?"

"Isn't it obvious? I am documenting the happy occasion."

Sugarbrook shook his head. "You're a wedding photographer."

"It's my job to get behind the scenes and under the skin of everyone here."

"Does this *look* like a wedding to you?"

"Well, that's the point, isn't it?" The photographer gave the DCI a wink. "Themed weddings. A break from the norm."

"I think you've got under enough people's skin now," Sugarbrook said. "Off you go."

"But... but..."

Sugarbrook raised an eyebrow. The photographer grunted and turned towards the door, spotting Diana.

He grinned. "What about this lovely lady? I see you as a supermodel who stepped back from the limelight to spend more time on the things that really matter in life. The patina of a few decades has only enhanced that superb bone structure and your radiant aura."

Diana smiled in spite of herself.

Sugarbrook stalked over, glaring as the photographer squeezed off a few final shots of Diana.

"Fine, I'm going!" The photographer took a couple more pictures as he backed away.

"How do we see the photos?" called Arwen.

The photographer whirled to face them. "Seriously, have they not shared the QR code with you? It was supposed to be displayed everywhere. One moment!"

He left the room and came back a few seconds later with a tea trolley.

"Here you go! This one has the code you need." He pointed to a laminated sheet taped to the end of the trolley. "Scan this baby and you'll get access to all of the pictures once I've popped them up into the cloud. Have a most enjoyable day, all of you. Even you, my gruffly powerful policeman."

He blew a kiss at Sugarbrook and scurried out.

The room was silent for a long moment. Diana could see that they were all stunned.

Lydia strode towards the trolley with the code. "Well, I want to see those photos." She grabbed the laminated sheet. "Ooh, there are fancy puddings on here!"

"I'm quite certain they're not intended for us," said Diana, but she was too late. The two groups began to descend on the trolley just as Penny Slipper barged in.

"Those are not for you!" she said, attempting to sweep in front of the dessert trolley.

She looked around to see the half-eaten platters of hors d'oeuvre on the other tables.

"What?"

She looked at Diana, who felt herself shrink back. She realised now that she should have warned the guests, but she'd been too busy in the interview cupboard.

"These need to be taken out of here!" Penny barked. "Now!"

Four members of waiting staff hurried into the room and began to take away the platters. Penny stood, arms stretched, warding off the bus tour guests while the half-empty platters were removed.

Diana watched as Penny took a breath, pulled on a thin smile, and turned to the guests.

"I'm sorry, but this food is not for you." She hesitated, opening and closing her mouth.

At last, she grunted. "It just isn't."

She hurried out of the room with a huff.

The two tour groups watched in stunned silence. First the photographer, then this.

Diana stepped forward and indicated the trolley that had been left with them.

"We've still got tea, coffee and biscuits," she said.
No one approached the trolley.

Chapter Eighteen

"Lush!" exclaimed Arwen, holding her phone in the air. "The photographer's uploaded the pictures. They are proper mint!"

Diana needed to understand what kind of mix-up had happened. She scanned the QR code with her phone, and found herself on a website for *Mel and Pete's wedding reception*, taking place today in one of the other function rooms.

"You can put in requests for the disco here," said one of the bridge group. "I've requested *I Gotta Feeling* by the Black Eyed Peas."

"Mate?" said Tom. "You do know that the disco thing isn't happening in here, don't you?"

"I know, but it's a great tune. They'll thank me for it."

Diana shook her head. She opened the gallery on her phone to see what pictures of herself had been uploaded.

"Hmm." They weren't bad at all: the man's eye for a picture was as good as his patter.

She looked up at her guests. "This is turning out to be the craziest of days."

"It's not how I saw today panning out, I've got to say," said Arwen, standing next to her near the tea trolley. "But at least I'm here, with my girls." She gave a little wave at the others.

"How often do you get to see your family?" Diana asked.

"Nowhere near as often as I should. Especially with mum's illness, I really should make more time for her." She shrugged. "You know how life gets in the way."

"I do. My own mother's only across town in Bow and I don't see her as often as I should."

"Well, that's why I've got Lydia."

"Pardon?"

Arwen looked at the glamorous middle-aged woman over by the window. "Lydia's my 'London Mum' cos my own one is so far away."

"Oh." Diana eyed the woman by the window. "And does your real mum know you call Lydia your 'London Mum'?"

Arwen tuned to her. "D'you think she'd mind?"

DCI Sugarbrook was behind them, cradling a cup filled a cup to the brim with black coffee.

"Right," he said, tersely. "If we can get on with this without further interruptions." He randomly pointed a finger at another guest. "You! In there."

By early evening, the police had interviewed only twelve of the twenty guests. Diana gathered the group together in the function room.

"I'm sorry our day has been interrupted by this sad turn of events," she said, "but I hope we'll be able to get back on track tomorrow."

"Will we get to see the bridges we missed today?" asked Stuart, the man dressed in tweed.

She smiled. "We'll make sure it's a jam-packed day for everyone."

"When we are done speaking to everyone," inserted DCI Sugarbrook. "Everyone is staying at this hotel, is that correct?"

"It is," said Diana.

"Then you will all *stay* at this hotel."

"Stay? Like prisoners?" asked Stuart.

"Did you have plans to be elsewhere?"

"No."

"Well, then. Good." He turned to Diana. "You and I will go to reception. I will collect room numbers. I will station officers in the lobby and I think you and I can say farewell for one day."

"It's been a busy day," she agreed.

He grunted. "Why do I get the impression that you attract trouble?"

"It is merely an impression, I can assure you."

They walked down to the reception to find Zaf chatting to Penny.

"Forensics are done at the depot," he said. "I see things have been a bit hectic here."

Diana looked at Penny; her face was pale and her shirt, normally so neat, was unbuttoned at the top with a stain on the arm.

"We've imposed too much," she said.

"It's not your fault," Penny said. "You'd think a wedding photographer could tell when he's not actually at a wedding. And as for the kitchen staff delivering the wedding buffet to the wrong room…"

"Oh dear," said Diana. "I'm so sorry our guests ate it."

"No. What gets me is that my manager doesn't see it for the accidental mix up it was."

"You're not in trouble, are you?"

Penny waved a hand in dismissal. "It's fine. Mr Carlton Lazar was causing me grief long before today."

"I can have a word with your manager if it would help," suggested Sugarbrook.

"I really don't think it will," Penny replied. "Best to let the whole thing drift from his memory. Will you still need the room tomorrow?"

Diana was about to suggest they could go elsewhere.

"That would be very helpful," said Sugarbrook. "I shall also post some plain clothes officers in this lobby if that's not a problem."

Penny gave a tired shrug. "If they could do some tidying while they're here, that would be a bonus."

Chapter Nineteen

Diana felt for Penny; she knew what it was like to have an overbearing boss. But there was little she could do to help.

She and Zaf left the Redhouse Hotel and took a slow walk back to their shared flat in in Pimlico. She was tired and barely noticed the shoppers on Oxford Street or the traffic at Marble Arch.

As they walked along Park Lane, she felt the openness of Hyde Park on their right start to soothe her nerves a little. She smiled as Zaf recounted his and Newton's attempts to distract Gus by creating a fake crime scene.

"I wish I'd been there to see Paul Kensington's face," she said.

"It was like this." Zaf turned to her and pulled an angry yet confused scowl.

She laughed. "And Newton was so wrapped up in what he was doing that he didn't even know Paul was there."

"That's Newton for you."

"It is."

They paused at Wellington Arch to cross the road.

"If we take all the stuff out of the office first thing," Zaf said, "I'm sure Paul will chalk it up to something the police were looking at."

Diana raised her eyebrows at the idea of Zaf being early for work, but said nothing. "I vote we grab something easy for dinner tonight. It's been a trying day."

"Good idea," said Zaf. "And we promised Alexsei we'd push on with Bryan's flat. It's so close to being done."

Diana nodded. She was lucky to be a long-term tenant in a flat in one of London's loveliest squares, on a peppercorn rent. Her upstairs neighbour, Bryan, had benefited from the same deal, but had passed away a few months ago. The flat was valuable and Alexsei's father, the owner, was eager to let it out again. Diana had persuaded him to let her and Zaf sort through Brian's possessions first.

"D'you find it weird?" Zaf asked as the emerged from the subway under Wellington Arch and passed building work on Grosvenor Place, the high walls of Buckingham Palace on their left. "I know you and Bryan went back a long way."

"Not weird exactly." Diana considered. "It's been more draining than I expected. He had so much stuff, and I want to deal with it in a way he'd have approved of. It gives me a chance to remember him. He would have loved seeing you wear his clothes."

Zaf smiled. He was wearing one of Brian's more subdued shirts under his Chartwell and Crouch blazer today. "He was clearly a man of great taste."

They stopped at Victoria Station to grab two ready meals from the branch of Marks and Spencer and picked up their pace to get home and eat.

In their kitchen, Zaf started heating things up in the

microwave. He pointed at the friendship contract on the fridge. "Thanks for having my back today."

They'd drawn up the friendship contract during the fraught early days of living together. Diana had rashly offered to help Zaf when he was homeless, and almost destroyed their burgeoning friendship. Simple things, like whose food was whose and how they should share the bathroom, had almost been their undoing.

Having each other's backs was one of their rules, but Diana wasn't sure what Zaf was referring to. "In what way?"

"I really thought the body had dropped off the bridge. You could have mocked me, but you just set me straight."

Diana frowned. "It was a horrible and confusing thing, Zaf. I'm not sure any of us made much sense of it. I hope the police can sort it out, and quickly."

"D'you think they will?"

Diana put down her fork and sighed.

"We have twenty people on our tour. Had, I suppose. The hen party all know each other, but the bridge guys... apart from a tight knot of friends around Tom Hatcher, they barely know each other. David Medawar, the dead man, knew no one apart from Tom, and they'd never met in the flesh before yesterday. David wasn't even into bridges. He was just someone who saw Tom's bridge project as an investment."

"What is this bridge project?"

"Something hi-tech. I don't know the details." She swallowed a mouthful of her pasta, thinking. "Now, everyone was at the hotel last night as Thursday night's stay was part of the tour package deal. What we do know – and I'm telling you something I overheard while sitting in on those interviews – is that David Medawar ended up having drinks with Gaynor and Bethan in the hotel restaurant. The mum and sister from the hen party."

Zaf nodded. "Gaynor's on chemo, right?"

"Right. And Bethan's got that broken arm. Her mum and DCI Sugarbrook both seem to think her boyfriend had something to do with that, although Bethan denies it. And Bethan claims Gaynor spent the evening boring David with the details of her cancer and treatment."

"I guess if you're that ill, it's all you can think about," said Zaf, chasing a lima bean around his plate.

"I don't doubt that. And Gaynor seems to have quite a sanguine attitude to it all."

"Sanguine. Good word."

She smiled. "I try. But as far as I know, they're the only people who interacted with David. I think he spent most of the tour this morning just reading his book."

"I saw that. The Agatha Christie."

"Yes. You ever read any of them?"

Zaf shook his head. "I've seen the films. The ones with, oh, thingy, Gilderoy Lockhart from Harry Potter."

"Kenneth Branagh."

"That's him. They're alright, I guess. Glitzy."

Diana stood up. "I've got some somewhere. You should read a couple." She stepped into the hallway and rummaged in the bookshelves next to the front door of her flat. A couple of minutes later, she returned and placed three books on the kitchen table.

"Christie had a gift for a plot twist, and in her later books, the psychology of crime. And she used her science background to make her murders believable."

She picked up the copy of *Sparkling Cyanide*.

"She wasn't from London but she had lots of connections

in the city. Her aunt, the inspiration for Miss Marple, lived in Ealing. And she learned about poisons while training at Apothecaries Hall in Blackfriars Lane."

Zaf picked up the copy of *The Murder on the Links*. "I'll give this one a try."

Diana nodded. "And there's a memorial statue to her on Cranbourn Street in the West End."

"Careful now," Zaf said. "Talk like that will have Paul Kensington having us delivering an Agatha Christie tour."

"I'd enjoy that."

"Yeah, but a typo would mean we end up delivering it alongside a Christian tour at the same time."

Diana laughed. "Murders and churches. Could be worse."

Zaf took their plates to the sink. "I'll go upstairs and make a start on Bryan's things."

Diana waved *Sparkling Cyanide* at him. "I'll be along in a minute. Mrs Christie and I might want to get reacquainted."

Chapter Twenty

Zaf was still getting used to how big the houses in Eccleston Square were. Tall houses with crazy high ceilings and rooms that went back and back. It was hard to imagine that this had once been a home for just one family. Well, one family and their servants. He had a good idea which of those he'd have been.

Each level was now a separate apartment, connected by a staircase far wider and more ornate than any modern staircase. Bryan's flat was on the second floor and over the last few months, Zaf had been helping Diana clear it out.

Zaf walked through the almost-empty space. He'd enjoyed the challenge of passing on some of Bryan's gorgeous belongings to people who'd appreciate them. An onyx chess set was wrapped up in bubble wrap, ready for an excited online buyer, and the half dozen or so remaining paintings were covered in protective blankets ready for moving.

Most of what was left was either very small or very big. Zaf and Diana had developed the habit of collecting crisp boxes from their local corner shop and filling them with fridge magnets, coasters and cocktail stirrers. Each time they filled one, they left it by the door for a trip to a charity shop.

This evening, Zaf was planning to look at Bryan's musical instruments, despite not knowing what half of them were. Bryan had been a session musician, and according to Diana, capable of getting a tune out of anything.

Somewhere out there was a home for each of these things. With a bit of research, Zaf would find those homes.

He pulled a mystery instrument down off a high shelf and dusted it before taking a photo. It looked like a violin that had been turned into a music box, with a little crank handle on the end.

He eyed it. What if it *was* just a fancy music box? He gave the handle a few turns and it emitted a hideous wailing sound.

He nearly dropped it in fright.

Who'd make a music box that wailed like that?

He put it on a table and leaned over it, trying to work out what it was supposed to be. He gave the handle another turn. More distorted wailing.

He was interrupted by a knock at Bryan's front door. "Hello?"

"Alexsei?" Zaf called. "I'm through here."

Alexsei put his head around the doorframe. "I heard a shrieking sound, like a little girl in pain." Zaf wished Alexsei would smile when he joked, so he could be sure the man *was* joking.

Alexsei was British-Azerbaijani and lived in the ground floor flat. He was young and as far as Zaf knew, wasn't actually the owner of the building, but looked after it for a wealthy father or uncle or someone.

Zaf looked down at the object on the table. "No idea

what it is. It made a right din when I turned the handle. It must be broken."

Alexsei picked it up. "Bryan had some interesting musical instruments." He took a seat and placed the instrument on his lap. His left hand went to the keys and his right turned the handle. He played a tune something like accordion music with a bagpipey overtone.

Zaf grinned. "You know how to play this thing? Does that mean you know what it is?"

"It is a Hurdy Gurdy. An instrument with a long and interesting history, but perhaps not so fashionable now."

"It's a string instrument, right? And yet the noise it makes sounds nothing like guitars or violins."

"It is because the instrument features drone strings. Even before you make the tune, they are playing. There is a wheel underneath this part here that sounds them." Alexsei pointed.

"Drone strings?"

"Constant sound, like the drone on a bagpipe. The Hurdy Gurdy would have been like a cheap-ass one-man band."

Zaf smiled. Sometimes Alexsei sounded like he had learned English from the world's finest language schools, with evening classes delivered by Samuel L Jackson. Probably just American TV.

"How d'you know about it?" he asked. "Hurdy Gurdy. Maddest name for an instrument ever."

"Hm." Alexsei nodded, his brow furrowed. "It is a name that speaks of the sound it makes, I think. Rhythmic and coarse. Hur-dy Gur-dy. Hur-dy Gur-dy." He mimed the cranking as he spoke.

"You're right," Zaf said.

"There are instruments in Bryan's collection that are less obscure." Alexsei put the Hurdy Gurdy back on the table and strode to a row of guitars on stands. "The guitars are the best of Bryan's instruments, I think. He used them a lot."

Zaf watched Alexsei run a hand across the guitars. Beside the ones out in the open were even more, still in their cases: twelve in total.

Alexsei picked an acoustic guitar off its rack and sat for a few moments adjusting the tuning. "I studied music when I was at UCL. Bryan was generous with his knowledge."

Alexsei strummed the guitar, an intensity in his eyes that drew Zaf in. People were shallow most of the time, but when Zaf looked at Alexsei's eyes, there was a depth, a hint of real substance inside. It made his skin tingle.

Chapter Twenty-One

Zaf didn't know the tune Alexsei was playing, but it somehow conjured summer nights and a sultry, lazy darkness.

The door opened and Diana entered. "Hello, both, nice to see you getting along."

Zaf and Alexsei exchanged a slightly panicked look.

"Yes, well," said Alexsei. "Your education must continue another time." He stood abruptly, put the guitar back on its stand and smiled at Diana before whirling out of the room.

Zaf watched him go. "Did I upset him?"

"Upset? No."

"He's so off with me at times."

She raised an eyebrow. "Hmm. Did I hear him playing Bryan's Hurdy Gurdy?"

"Did you know what it was called?"

"Yes."

Zaf huffed with frustration. "It's been driving me mad not even knowing what to call them, and it turns out the house is full of people who know."

"We should always aim for better communication," said Diana. It was a quote from their friendship contract on the fridge downstairs.

Zaf tapped the piano stool in front of Bryan's piano. "I don't understand why you don't swap this piano stool for the one by your dressing table. It's got a lift-up seat with storage, and you can never have too much storage."

Diana lifted the lid to find sheet music. "You make a very good point."

"OK. I'll carry it down while you take photos of the obscure instruments and text me the photos with their names."

"Deal."

Zaf carried the piano stool down to Diana's room in their flat. He set it down in front of her dressing table, pleased to see it looked much better there than her old stool.

He didn't often enter Diana's room, and couldn't resist a look around. There were three massive wardrobes, big enough to be portals to Narnia. The bed had a faded green quilt that Diana called an eiderdown, whatever that was. But its shabby style suited the room.

The dressing table was cluttered with pots, bottles and products that Zaf was about to examine when he spotted something more interesting. Beside the bed was small bookcase, holding what looked like journals, each labelled with its year.

"The infamous Diana diaries," he muttered.

He couldn't resist walking over and taking a closer look, resisting the urge to touch.

He peered at the spine of one. "The year two thousand," he said, in a deep voice like a narrator in a cheesy old sci-fi movie.

He reached out a hand and the journal slipped off the shelf and fell open on the floor.

Zaf felt his heart flutter. He looked up at the door. He shouldn't be hanging around in here. He shouldn't be prying.

But...

He recognised Diana's writing on the open pages.

A busy few days! Went to Reading Festival with Justine F. Elastica's set was great. Spent some time with the singer from a US band called Black Eyed Peas who wanted my combat jacket, but I said no.

New restaurant opened in Kensington called Beetroot Beetroot! *Pascal asked me to go with him (that's become a regular thing now) and we had the tasting menu. Foie gras mousse, followed by duck breast. We were just talking and talking and it was like the years of separation just hadn't happened. By the end of the night my head was spinning.*

"Ooh hello," Zaf muttered. "A boyfriend?"

Diana had never mentioned past loves, and he knew she'd never been married. But he couldn't believe such a sociable and outgoing woman wouldn't have had a boyfriend or girlfriend or two in her decades on this planet.

His gaze skated past talk of food and wine. He wanted more of the gossip.

Finally got a pair of Ugg boots. I can see why everyone raves about them.

. . .

"Really?" Had Diana really worn those clumpy boots? They just looked like big slippers to him.

Pascal wants to go for brunch on Sunday. He knows I can't resist a Bucks Fizz on a sunny day. Le Jardin Enchanté in Holland Park, not far from the Mews where he lives. Tara Palmer-Tomkinson goes there. She told me it's a velour tracksuit kind of place, relaxed and informal.

Zaf grimaced. "Velour tracksuit! Ugh."

It was unavoidable that talk turned to Ariadne. Things are not good between them. He can't trust her to be honest and insightful, which, apparently, is how he views me. He says he needs me. He watches me drink, looking for every movement on my face. How can he do what he does without someone like me? He needs me.

The wine was a jazzy Vinho Verde with spiky fruit tones. That was the description we settled on.

Two diary entries for the mysterious Pascal! Zaf's mind was racing. Who was he? Was Diana still in touch with him?

There was the sound of the flat door opening.

He slammed the diary shut and put it back on the shelf, careful to place it exactly where it had been.

He hurried to the stool, making a show of adjusting it and patting it down.

"Yes," he called out, "I think this would be just right here."

"Glad to hear it," Diana called back.

Chapter Twenty-Two

When Zaf woke up on Saturday morning, he felt as if his sleeping brain had been trying to organise him.

His mind had fed him a dream in which he'd had to explain himself to unseen judges. No, not unseen judges. High above him, a giant version of Gus the cat had been sitting on the edge of the upper deck of the open-top bus, throwing yellow scenes of crime markers down at him every time he tried to explain himself. Each of the little markers had a score on it, as if Zaf was an ice-skating or ballroom dancing contestant. The scores weren't high.

As Zaf cleansed his face in the bathroom mirror, he was left with the sense that he should try harder in life and be generally better.

"A better version of you," he told his reflection.

He wanted a better version of himself that knew more, like what a 'hurdy-gurdy' was. A better version of himself that had plans for the future and could look the likes of Alexsei in the eye with confidence.

He peered into the mirror. Why did he keep thinking about Alexsei? The man was just his landlord. Well, Diana's landlord really. Not even that. Diana's landlord's son.

But Zaf somehow cared what Alexsei thought of him. He wanted to get past the cold disdain Alexsei had shown him when he'd first moved in. He wanted Alexsei to stop seeing him as a threat to Diana. And, he had to admit, he wanted Alexsei to like him.

Zaf saw himself blushing in the mirror. Truth, Alexsei was hot. Who wouldn't want him to like them?

"The boy's cute," he told his reflection and raised an eyebrow. He lowered it and pat-dried his face dry on a towel.

The world was full of cute men. That Tom Hatcher, the bridge guy in the amazing shirt, had been throwing him flirty signals. Zaf would happily flirt with Tom if he couldn't get the attention of coldly distant Mr Dadashov.

But he needed to make some improvements in his life if he was going to progress and grow. If he wanted to be a better tour guide, if he wanted to further his career, if he wanted the likes of Alexsei to take him more seriously...

Zaf needed to stop being that shallow fun-loving guy whose only contributions to the world were a series of banal social media posts.

"You've got to be a better you," he told himself, again.

He left his bedroom to find that Diana had already set out for the day. Nothing unusual there; she'd be out in the square, tending the gardens of empty houses.

He glanced at her bedroom door.

Those diaries were so tempting...

No. It's prying.

She'd never know.

He nipped into her room and slipped the year two thousand off the shelf again.

Almost immediately, he found a reference to this possible boyfriend, Pascal.

Seeing Pascal tomorrow. A three course catered 'boutique picnic' with accompanying wines. Can't wait!

The following day had more detail.

I met Pascal at his place. He's fastened a wonky horseshoe over his door for luck. He's quite superstitious. Ariadne is away with ACE. He's more relaxed without her around. I think he's told her about us. Well, we've been doing this, night after night, for months now. How could she not know?

"Scandalous, Diana!" Zaf whispered.

We caught the tube to the launch event and were shown to our blanket. There was a low table for the food and drink, and we lounged in the sunshine on Primrose Hill dining like kings.

There was potted crab to start, then hot smoked salmon salad. It's not often I go crazy for sides, but there was a sweet red onion pickle that I couldn't get enough of. Pascal laughed at me scraping out the last of it with my finger!

I sampled all of the wines, naturally. The champagne was

decent enough. There was a gorgeous Soave, like summer in a glass.

We stayed for hours. An afternoon I won't forget in a hurry.

Zaf smiled. "A boutique picnic." It sounded like the most romantic meal imaginable.

We had the radio for background music. I nearly died when Count Me In *came on. It doesn't get a lot of airplay these days, even if it did reach number three back in the day. How many people can say they've been in the top five?*

Zaf frowned.

Top five? What was Diana talking about?

He scanned the rest of the page, but the rest of it was about chatting to some people at the picnic.

He needed more information about *Count Me In*. He drummed his fingers on the hard cover of the journal, thinking. If she'd been part of a recording, she might have mentioned it earlier in her diary.

He went to the start and flicked through, alert for *Count Me In*.

There!

In January there was an entry mentioning the song.

Morris asked me at work today if I'd ever consider going back into the music biz. Clearly managing the Chartwell and

Crouch team isn't enough for him. He's composed something new and wants to release it. It's no Count Me In *but it's pretty catchy. Then he said he was thinking about getting the old gang back together. He meant Pascal and Ariadne. I had to remind him that the four of us are barely talking (well, apart from my secret meet-ups with Pascal). Morris thinks he's going to get us back together. Yeah, we'll see...*

Zaf heard a sound outside the door and dropped the book, his heart hammering. He picked it up with a swift motion and replaced it, then hurried out of the room.

The flat was empty. He'd been imagining things.

Still... He should stop snooping.

As he walked past the garden at the centre of their square, he remembered that tomorrow was Diana's birthday, the day of the barbecue. A new and improved Zaf would do something significant to help Diana celebrate her big day.

A new and improved Zaf would do something to make his mark on the world every day.

Diana had said that a diary was a good way to measure progress. The mother of the bride, Gaynor, was also a diary-keeper. Maybe it helped as she struggled with her illness.

Zaf wasn't sure he had the discipline to keep a diary. He might start one, but it would soon peter out.

He made a decision as he approached the bus stop. He should simply focus on each day as it came, not be too ambitious.

Hopefully they'd be able to take their group to Tower Bridge today, so he should learn some facts and figures. He'd have more authority if he could reel things off the way Diana did.

He googled some key dates and facts on his phone as he rode the number 2 bus from Vauxhall Bridge Road to Gloucester Place, and tested himself on them as he walked along Dorset Street to the bus depot.

Inside the depot, there was no sign the forensics team had ever been there. And the tape and marks had been cleared away from the fake crime scene in Paul Kensington's office.

He spotted movement on the top deck of the open top bus and climbed up the stairs at the back.

"Morning," he said.

Newton looked back towards him. He was working his way along the deck with a huge cloth and an old tin of metal polish, rubbing the metal headrests to a brilliant shine.

"Morning."

"Removing every trace," Zaf said.

"Huh?"

"Of the forensic team's work."

"Oh. Yeah. Yeah."

Gus was on a seat near Newton. He stood on his hind legs and tapped the nearest headrest: *here, do this bit*. Newton dutifully polished.

"We'll make it so the customers don't even know there was a murder up here," said Newton, not looking up.

Zaf looked around. "Maybe we should stick this tour group on another bus for the rest of the weekend."

Newton paused. "Really?"

"I don't think any amount of polishing and cleaning is going to stop this being the *death bus*. Not for this group, at least."

Newton gestured over at the other two buses. "But the others aren't open-top."

"So they'll definitely know it's a different bus, which is a good thing."

"Well, of course they're different," said Newton, his brow furrowed. "This is an RM1414, very different to RM2760 over there. Three feet difference in length, for one thing."

Zaf smiled. "I think most customers will only really notice that that one's got a roof and the other doesn't."

Newton looked unconvinced. "You're really sure we should use a different bus?"

"Trust me."

Zaf glanced at the seat halfway along the top deck where David Medawar had sat. Someone had strangled him in that seat. Someone had come up here while everyone else was downstairs and throttled the man to death.

He shivered. "That guy David was strangled with a strap or a rope or something."

"Is that so?" Newton replied.

"How would someone even do that?" Zaf imagined wrapping a rope around someone's neck and pulling. "It'd take a lot of strength."

Newton grunted. "I don't know. With the right leverage... If I was going to strangle someone up here..."

"Yes?"

"I'd do it from behind." He placed his hands on the shoulders of an imaginary person sitting in one of the seats. "It would be easier if they didn't expect me."

Newton sat down behind the imaginary person. "If you threw the rope around their neck and pulled, they'd be forced back against the back of the seat. In fact..." He threaded his hands through the metal headrest. "If you somehow got your rope through here, then the person would be garrotted between rope and headrest, with no possibility of moving away."

Zaf rubbed his own throat. "Eeesh. That's... that's horrible."

Newton shrugged. "That's how I'd do it."

Chapter Twenty-Three

Diana hadn't been tending the gardens in the square after all. Instead, she had walked straight from her flat to the Redhouse Hotel.

"Morning, Penny," she said. "Our guests still at breakfast?"

Penny gave her a thin smile and gestured towards the hotel restaurant.

"What's wrong?" Diana asked. Penny was normally so full of sparkle.

"Oh, it's nothing. A couple of scheduling problems yesterday caused me some difficulty."

Diana thought back to the incident with the wedding photographer. "Was it our group?"

Penny gave a small shrug. "It really wasn't anybody's fault. Wrong place, wrong time. Wrong food, wrong photographer."

"You got into trouble for that?"

A small nod.

Diana leaned over the reception desk. "I'm so very sorry, Penny. That's unfair, with everything you do to help people."

"It's fine, really. Water under the bridge."

Diana gave Penny an apologetic smile then made for the restaurant. The Chartwell and Crouch groups weren't hard to spot. A bunch of men sat at a table by the window, laughing over their coffees. The women had found a longer table where they could sit together.

As she speared fruit segments with her fork, Arwen flicked through one of the hotel's fashion magazines, showing pictures to Lydia opposite. Gaynor sat two seats along, wearing a different wig from the one she'd sported the previous day, but equally stylish. She looked agitated.

Diana approached her. "Is everything alright?"

Bethan looked up from rooting in the carrier bag that Gaynor had been given as a temporary replacement for her bag. "Mum's lost her diary."

"Sorry to hear that," Diana said. "Can you describe it for me?"

"It's the size of an exercise book." Gaynor used her hands to indicate the size. "Bright purple cover. I've never lost it before."

"We can all keep a look out. It's sure to be in the hotel if you had it yesterday." Diana reached into a carrier bag she'd brought from home. "But I've brought you this." She pulled out a handbag from her own collection.

Gaynor's eyes widened. "For me?"

"Until the police return your other one."

"That's a Hermès Constance!" said Lydia.

"Is it?" said Diana, pretending not to know. "It was just lying around the house."

"It's roomy," said Gaynor. "Enough to fit my vitamin smoothie bottle in."

"Drink up before you put that bottle anywhere," Bethan said. "We've got a long day ahead of us."

Lydia leaned over to Gaynor and lowered her voice. "Have you any idea how much one of those bags is worth?"

Diana retreated, happy to have brought a smile to the face of one of her guests.

She returned to reception to find both Zaf and DCI Sugarbrook at the desk.

"Will the group be at liberty to continue their tour today?" she asked the detective.

"You and I both know there are several interviews still outstanding, Miss Bakewell. Let's see how the day progresses, but for now, I'd like them where I can easily reach them."

Diana sighed. The group wouldn't be happy.

She looked from Sugarbrook to Penny. "We'll need to ask Penny here if she can spare us a room."

Penny's face dropped into a frown, quickly replaced by a professional smile. She eyed the DCI.

"Mr Lezar – my manager – was unhappy with some aspects of yesterday. We can't have any more mix-ups with food trolleys."

Sugarbrook gave her a nod. "I'm sure your guests are grateful for your efforts."

Diana wasn't so sure. The tour group were frustrated at being cooped up, and probably didn't even appreciate that they'd been spared a trip to the police station.

Penny consulted her screen. "You can use the same room again for your interviews."

"Cupboard," said Sugarbrook.

A shrug. "Cupboard. And function room three will be clear until five."

Sugarbrook grunted. "That will have to do. Thank you."

Diana went off to start gathering the members of the two groups. They were far from happy at the news.

Arwen huffed loudly. "Mum could have stayed in Wales if she was just going to sit around all day."

But Gaynor didn't seem irritated: too busy exploring her temporary handbag.

"Another day without bridges," grunted Stuart. "I'm keeping count."

Zaf put on a smile. "Ah, but we have a very different day lined up. I hope you're ready for some excitement!"

There were a few groans and much eye rolling.

Chapter Twenty-Four

Once Zaf and Diana had gathered everyone together in the function room, Diana went off to help with the interviews.

Zaf watched as the two groups withdrew to opposite corners of the room. He scratched his nose, thinking of ways to help them get through the day.

Let's try the hen party first.

"OK," he said as he approached them, "I want to do some information gathering. Can you tell me three things you all enjoy as a group?" He slapped a piece of paper and a pen down for them. "Confer amongst yourselves, I'll be back in a minute."

He walked over to the bridge group. "How about this group? Three things you all enjoy as a group?"

Ten minutes later he had two pieces of paper with ideas written on them. He read through them.

"Sorry folks, we can't do anything involving alcohol. DCI Sugarbrook won't be happy if he's interviewing you drunk.

And I'll discard anything relating to your tour, because we *will* get back to that, whatever happens."

He raised an eyebrow and looked around the groups. "That leaves us with two activities. I think it's fair to say these will take some of you out of your comfort zone, but in a good way."

There was low-level grumbling.

"What d'you say? Are we all gonna give it a go?"

"I'm really not sure—" one of the men began.

Tom elbowed him in the ribs. "Give over, Craig. It won't kill us to join in." He gave Zaf a thumbs-up. "Count us in!"

Zaf looked around. "Right, we have two activities, one nominated by each group. I'll toss a coin to choose which one we tackle first."

He fished out a coin and flipped it, catching it on the edge of his hand.

"Heads. That means we will spend the first session engaged in a... wait for it... fashion show!"

The men's expressions hovered between horror and embarrassed interest.

"The number one rule," said Zaf, "is that we can't leave the room, so we're going to have to model whatever we can find in here. I want to be wowed by your creativity and style."

"How about we make the catwalk and they make the fashion show?" asked Bunty.

Zaf gave him a look. "Absolutely not. *I* will make a catwalk. Form your teams. They don't have to be your existing groups. I expect everybody to take turns as a model."

"Well, this is ridiculous!" said Stuart. "I'm not doing it."

"Then let's interview you first," Sugarbrook called over from the cupboard door.

"Gladly," Stuart huffed.

"Don't worry, cuz," Tom shouted. "I'll fashion you a costume!" He grinned at Zaf.

Zaf smiled back. "You've got an hour to prepare. Now, go!"

Chapter Twenty-Five

"Stuart Dinktrout, is it?" asked Sugarbrook as the interviewee settled into his seat next to Diana.

"Of Dinktrout Nurseries," Stuart replied. "Home of the famous Dinktrout Rose."

"Right."

"You've heard of it?"

Sugarbrook wrinkled his nose. "I'm not much of a gardener."

Stuart looked at Diana, squeezed in beside him in the interview cupboard. "*You've* heard of it?"

"Is that the one with the coloured edges, white and red?" she asked.

Stuart looked back at Sugarbrook. "See? She knows. Famous."

"Very good."

Stuart continued to gesture at Diana. "Why is she here? Isn't she just the tour guide?"

Sugarbrook tried to hide his smile. "Yes, she is."

"Does she have to be here?"

"She certainly does not." The DCI gave Diana a thin smile. "Perhaps, Miss Bakewell, you are no longer needed."

Diana shrugged and rose from her chair.

"No," said Stuart. "Wait. Why did everyone else yesterday get to have her here and I don't?"

Sugarbrook looked at him. "You just said—"

"I'm not being deprived of something everyone else has."

Sugarbrook sighed and indicated for Diana to sit again. He consulted his notes.

"So, you were booked onto the bridge sightseeing tour."

"I was," replied Stuart, "although I've already noticed we missed some."

"The intention is to circle back and make sure we do all of them," Diana put in.

He narrowed his eyes. "I've been counting."

Diana gave a small smile. "I've noticed."

"Big bridge fan, huh?" said Sugarbrook.

Stuart Dinktrout scoffed. A man like Stuart Dinktrout could dismiss the entire world with a single scoff.

"Bloody boring things, aren't they?" he said. "They're bridges. You put them up, they stay up. They do their damned job. Oh, credit and all that to those Victorian engineers. Those chaps knew what they were doing. And, yes, maybe I'm looking forward to seeing the insides of Tower Bridge. If we're ever allowed out of this place to go see it." He gave both Sugarbrook and Diana a pointed look. "But, no, not my cup of tea. Be happy enough when this weekend is over and I can get back to my dear Arabella."

"I see," said Sugarbrook, "so, that sort of begs the question—"

"Tom is my cousin," Stuart said. "Most of us are here because he invited us. He's a bit of a snowflake. Ugh. But apart from that, Tom seems to have his head screwed on. So I agreed to be an initial investor in his Bifrost project."

"Bifrost," said Sugarbrook. Detective Sergeant Quigley slid a piece of paper in front of him. "Ah. The bridge project."

"Tom's an engineer and he's got this superb bridge concept that he hopes to sell to the military."

"Right."

Stuart leaned forward. "In truth, the original idea was mine. Tom had come down to visit his mother. She's got a place in Stowmarket. I offered to help her with the design of her garden but she wants to make her mistakes all by herself. Anyway, I got chatting to Tom and he was working on some concepts and I happened to mention how climbing plants bridge gaps, you know, by growing out a single tendril to the next secure object and then growing thicker runners along the original. I could tell he was taken by it. The little cogs were turning in his mind. My idea but I've let him have it." He leaned back, beaming. "I'm generous like that."

"Generous, yes," said Sugarbrook. "But you invested money in it."

"I can always spot a winner. Yes, he struggled with all the prototypes but he's come through in the end. He's got a meeting with this Catherine Garrett woman, big cheese at an engineering company. Going to sign on the dotted line, turn it over to army chaps and the money will start rolling in."

"David Medawar was another investor. Did you know him well?"

"The dead chap?" Stuart shook his head. "Met him for the first time on Thursday night."

"You talked?"

"If you can call it talking. Some people today have no

personality. Like me, he was much more interested in the business side of things. Wanted to know how much I'd invested, a bit crass if you ask me. But he didn't want to talk long. He was on his way somewhere."

"On his way where?"

Stuart shrugged. "Had a book in his hand and was reading it like he was swotting up for a test or something. Like..." he frowned. "He was drinking it all in, this book, like he had to read it all before he got to where he was going."

"This book," said Sugarbrook. "What kind of book? Was it a novel?"

"No, no. Hardback. I didn't see it clearly. I wasn't all that interested."

"And what time was this?"

Another shrug. "Half-ten, maybe eleven."

"In the evening? So, at half past ten on the Thursday evening, David Medawar was leaving the hotel to go somewhere?"

Stuart shook his head. "He wasn't leaving the hotel. He was going to the lifts. He was going to a room."

"His room?"

"Definitely not the impression I got. I'm not sure he specifically said he was going to meet someone, but that was very much the impression I got. You know how it is, you're a policeman. You must pick up on the signals people give. He didn't actually say it, but there was a definite sense that he was going to meet someone in their room. A lady. Having said that, if you'd asked me, I'd have said he wasn't into women. You know the sort. Not that I've anything against the gays. Our Tom's one, for starters."

"Thank you," said Sugarbrook. "You've been very helpful."

Chapter Twenty-Six

Despite Zaf's suggestion that they mingle, the two groups had remained resolutely apart, forming two teams and split perfectly between men and women, bridge fans and Bridget fans. Each group was at one end of the room, conferring.

Zaf had done his best not to look at their preparations for the fashion show, preferring to keep it a surprise. He'd laid out a cat walk and kept an eye on the time, only shouting out to give them a ten-minute warning.

While he waited, he did some more research into Diana's supposed music career. He smiled when he found a refence on Wikipedia.

ElectraBeat, a pioneering English synth-pop band founded in London in 1977, had their commercial breakthrough with their second album, "Tantalise," in 1981. This record boasted several singles, most notably "Count Me In," which reached number three in the UK charts. The 1980s saw a stream of singles from the band, solidifying their status as influential synth-pop trailblazers.

Lead singer and producer Morris Walker was the sole constant band member from their inception in 1977 until their disbandment in 1987. Walker played a pivotal role in transforming ElectraBeat into a commercially successful act. During their peak years, the band featured keyboardist Ken Ferrari and female backing vocalists Ariadne Webb and Diana Bakewell.

There it was, plain as day. Diana had been a bona fide pop star. Well, a backing singer. But... wow!

Zaf was so excited, he almost forgot to stop the fashion show preparations. He realised time had overrun and stood up.

"Time everybody! Are we ready for the show?"

There were squeaks of protest and a few quick moves to add finishing touches.

"I suggest each group assembles as an audience for the other group's show. I will judge which is the best."

"Is there a prize for the best?" called Bunty.

"A prize?"

"I bet twenty quid we'll beat you," Bethan called over to the men.

"Bethan!" said her mum reproachfully.

"A twenty-pound bet?" said Bunty. "You're on."

"Fifty quid," she countered.

"Twenty's more than enough," said Zaf. "I've put out seating for you. I'll flip a coin to decide who goes first."

He flipped his coin while everyone watched.

Zaf looked up, smiling. "It's the Bridget Jones group first, who are apparently now called Team Hen. Gents, can I invite you to take your seats while they prepare to wow us with their show?"

There was much shuffling and scraping of chairs, while the women clustered in preparation.

"We've got music to accompany our show," said Arwen. "I'm gonna play it on my phone, so please everyone, be quiet."

"Pretty sure you can play it on the room's speakers," said Bunty, beckoning her over. "Give me a moment to get you logged in."

He fiddled with her phone and moments later music was reverberating through the room.

"Oh cool, thank you!" said Arwen, shouting to be heard. "It's a playlist that echoes our theme of stormy weather."

Lydia was first down the catwalk, to the tune of *Crying in the Rain*. Her outfit was an acid-coloured cagoule that had been somehow adjusted.

Zaf leaned forward to see how it had changed. The women must have had a tiny sewing kit with them: they'd made pleats and tucks in the baggy garment so that it sat across Lydia's body in sharp, avant-garde angles. Her upper torso formed a circular shape: was that a plate they'd sewn in?

Zaf smiled, leaning back in his chair. The look reminded him of Bertie Bassett.

Lydia twirled and preened a little then moved off to the side for the next person.

Gaynor was next. She moved slowly, as Zaf had seen her do before, but she stepped in time and held herself erect. She, too, wore a cagoule-based outfit, along with a dramatic headdress. An inverted ice cream cone, with wafty drapes hanging down: a fairytale princess kind of thing, Zaf thought.

This one definitely had an umbrella somewhere in its ancestry. It was an effective look.

"Good hat!" he called.

Gaynor gave him a shy smile and stood aside as another of the women, Phoebe, strode up.

Her outfit was a striking blue mac with a military look and an eighties silhouette. Were those wellies stuffed inside her coat, across her shoulders? The outfit even had epaulettes: bright yellow gloves, held onto the shoulders with staples or maybe stitches.

The music changed to *It's Raining Men* as Arwen made her appearance. She had a pale cagoule covered with generous folds of flowing, bridal white cotton. It hung from every part of her, and she even pulled a huge train along the floor, the entire length of the catwalk.

Zaf applauded. "Wow!"

How had they done that?

He glanced around the room and gasped. They'd used tablecloths. Tablecloths belonging to the hotel.

It looked stunning, but a small queasy part of him knew that this was bad, very bad.

The women concluded their show and stood in a line, all angular stances and pouting expressions. Zaf stood and applauded them long and hard. The men from the bridge group joined in.

"I think we can all agree that was a triumph! Well done to all of you. Let me take a picture of you all."

Zaf took pictures of them as a group and individually.

"Please take your seats now. It's time for our second

group to show us what they've got. Team Bridge, take it away!"

Tom waved towards the interview cupboard. "We're missing Stuart."

"He's not been here to make an outfit," Zaf said.

"Doesn't mean we haven't made one for him."

Whether the people inside had overheard or it was just a coincidence, the interview cupboard door opened and Stuart stepped out.

The men stood and formed a brief huddle. A few moments later, the speakers vibrated to *Burning Love* by Elvis.

The show was headed up by Tom. Somehow his outstretched arms had been made incredibly long, each draped in white, giving him the look of a religious icon.

Zaf groaned: more of the tablecloths.

There was a small clattering sound as Tom walked past, and Zaf caught a glimpse of a folded trestle table under his outfit, which explained how his armspan was so vast.

He gave a slow twirl, forcing Zaf to duck. Once Tom had completed his parade, he stood on show, although his expression suggested he'd have preferred to put the trestle table down.

Another man, Farhan, was next. Zaf shuffled forward to get a better view of the structure Farhan wore across his head and shoulders. He was dressed all in white, another tablecloth.

"No," Zaf muttered. This tablecloth had a hole in it, for Farhan's head.

They were going to be in so much trouble...

Across the man's shoulders and over his head was something that looked like a suspension bridge made out of spoons. It was cleverly constructed, with little white ties at each intersection.

Zaf wondered how many spoons the hotel had, and how many of them were currently sitting on Farhan's shoulders.

Farhan finished his parade and took his place next to Tom, hands on hips.

"Give us a hand with this table will you?" Tom hissed. "It's really heavy."

All eyes were now on Bunty.

"Can I please ask you to pull on the rope?" Bunty called to Zaf.

"Rope?"

Zaf's looked down to see a ragged rope leading along the floor. He picked up an end, hoping it wasn't a torn-up tablecloth knotted together, but knowing deep down that it was.

He pulled on the rope and realised it was attached to the tea trolley, which was now Bunty's chariot. The man sat on top of it, draped in white, with a shiny silver headdress that might have been the base of the water jug. He was swaddled in ten or more tablecloths, hanging to the floor down the sides of the trolley.

Zaf was relieved when Bunty reached the end of the catwalk and he could stop pulling the rope.

"And turn me round, if you'd be good enough!" Bunty called.

Zaf turned him around and then parked him at the end of the line with the rest of his group.

There was a loud clatter as Tom dropped the trestle table. Stuart and Tom howled in pain as it landed on their feet. Bunty looked on, smug to escape injury.

Zaf stood back and clapped. "Bravo! Can I check your

toes aren't broken or anything? If you're fine I'll take your photo."

When they'd composed themselves, Zaf grabbed his phone for photos. They hadn't all been models, but then he'd never really expected them to.

Tom held up the table, helped discreetly by the others to avoid accidents.

"Great work everybody," Zaf said. "Now I'll work out the final marks, so please take your seats and be ready for my announcement."

Chapter Twenty-Seven

Zaf scribbled on a piece of paper. Once he was satisfied with his thoughts, he stood and addressed the audience.

"I have awarded points in the following categories. First of all, best use of available materials, where I have rewarded creative re-use but deducted points for anything that caused damage to property. Team Hen score seven out of ten and Team Bridge score five out of ten."

There were howls of outrage from both teams.

Zaf held up a hand.

"Next category is style and visual impact. This one was a toughie because both teams excelled, so Team Hen score eight points... and Team Bridge score eight points as well."

The teams were quiet, each eyeing the other, eager to hear what came next.

"Our final category is the performance of your catwalk show. For this I have awarded six points to Team Hen and seven points to Team Bridge. So Team Hen have a one-point lead."

The Hens whooped and cheered, while the Bridge team hollered and protested that they'd been robbed.

"Pay up!" Bethan called to Bunty, her face alight with glee.

"It's definitely all to play for in the next round," said Zaf.

Bethan's face fell. "Next round?"

"The bet is not yet concluded," said Bunty.

Zaf nodded. "Our second challenge of the day. But before that can begin, can we possibly have a tablecloth amnesty? I want them all folded and piled up neatly. Make it look like we never touched them, please."

DS Quigley had crossed the room and was whispering in Bunty's ear. Bunty followed the sergeant to the interview cupboard.

"You're going to be one man down, chaps," he called.

"I think we'll cope!" replied Tom.

He grinned at Bunty, then flashed the last of the grin at Zaf.

Zaf felt warmth run through him.

Focus, he told himself. *You've got a job to do.* This wasn't exactly regular tour guide work, but at least the punters were enjoying themselves.

Soon enough, three piles of tablecloths were arranged in front of him. The first would pass as clean. He smoothed them flat as he re-folded them. Would they be OK to put on a table at an event? He hoped so.

The second pile of tablecloths were intact but dirty. He tried brushing off the dirt so that they could join the clean ones, but there were footprints, streaks of stubborn dust and even some inexplicable stains that looked like they might be chocolate.

He hoped it was chocolate.

The third pile was little more than tattered remains. These cloths had been cut and torn to make outfits. He had no idea how many the groups had used: right now, they looked like rags.

"We need ideas, people," he said. "We can't do this to the hotel staff. Penny downstairs has put herself out for us, and she'll get into trouble if we leave her with this mess."

"Sorry," said Lydia. "We got caught up in the challenge."

"It was like being on one of those telly programmes," said Gaynor, "where you have to make something out of junk."

Tom shrugged. "I think we were all just lost in the moment."

Zaf held up a handful of torn fragments. "So what do we do now?"

Gaynor raised a hand. "We've got three options. Hide the evidence and pretend this never happened; come clean and explain ourselves; or try and fix it."

There were murmurs of agreement. People shouted out suggestions.

Zaf held up his hands to silence them all. "First up, there's no fixing this. The tablecloth that got torn up to make this rope is a distant memory. Hotels like their tablecloths to look immaculate."

Stuart raised a mug and tapped it with a pen to gain attention. "The most obvious solution is surely to bribe a maid to make this all go away."

Zaf rocked backwards in his chair, pondering. "Or maybe, with the clean pile, we can just pretend that nothing ever happened. We leave them here as if we never touched them. With the dirty pile, we see if one of the staff can get them to the laundry and exchange them for clean ones."

"Bribe a maid, just as I suggested!" Stuart nodded, looking pleased with himself.

"*Not* as you suggested. We're not going to bribe anyone, mainly because we haven't got a big wodge of cash."

"Speak for yourself."

Arwen banged the table for attention. "We made this mess in the first place, and I don't like the word bribe."

"It's a dirty word," Tom agreed.

"So how about we re-jig the whole bribery idea?"

"Re-jig?" said a hen party member.

"In our heads, at least," said Arwen. Do we know the cleaning staff here?"

"I know the one who helped yesterday was Carmen," said Zaf.

Arwen surveyed the group. "Between us we must have something Carmen would like? Let's all turn out our pockets and figure out what that might be. Then we can invite this Carmen to collaborate with us?"

"Oh, *collaborate*," said Tom. "A much more palatable word."

"Either that or we just leave a bunch of ripped up tablecloths in the corner and declare that it's not our problem."

Zaf wanted to object to this, to point out that Arwen was still suggesting bribery, just by a different name.

But... it did sound more palatable. He decided to go along with the idea.

"Fine," he said. "What have we got? Let's pool our resources right here on the table."

Five minutes later, he shook his head in disappointment, poking at the sparse collection on the table.

"So we've got a part-used packet of chewing gum, a bottle of hand sanitiser, a key chain shaped like Malta and a book of four stamps. Are any of these objects going to be irresistible to Carmen?"

"I bet Bunty Jimjams has actually got a big wad of cash on him," said Tom.

"Twenty quid of which is mine," said Bethan.

Zaf looked around the group. Why was he wasting time on people's pocket rubbish?

But he wasn't about to beg posh Bunty for some cash.

"You know what?" he said. "I'm just going to talk to Carmen."

Chapter Twenty-Eight

"It strikes me, Mr Gieves-Jervois —" said Sugarbrook.

"It's Gieves-Jervois," said Bunty.

"Isn't that what I said?" said Sugarbrook.

"It's a soft 'g', an 'ay' sound after the 'j' and a hard 's'. Look, everyone calls me Jimjams. Bunty Jimjams."

Bunty smiled affably, his mouth full of slightly mismatched teeth.

"Bunty isn't your real name?" said Sugarbrook.

"Lord, no. Pet name given to me by Nanny." The smile broadened. "I was her special little lamb."

"Er, right."

Diana prided herself on having met and known people from all layers of society. Men like Bunty lived lives a million miles away from those of most other people, yet they were as capable of both human and inhuman behaviour as anyone else.

In fact, on first impressions, Diana rather liked Bunty Jimjams. He acted like a man who was just passing through the world, or maybe floating above it, and had decided to be polite and friendly as he did so.

"As I was saying," said Sugarbrook, "it strikes me... *Sir*, that you, Mr Dinktrout and Tom Hatcher, are perhaps the only people in your half of the group that actually know one another."

Bunty stuck out a bottom lip as he pondered this.

"Not strictly true. I know Alfie from the club. But generally, most of the chaps are complete strangers to one another. I don't think any of us personally knew the late David Medawar."

"Then can you suggest why he would have invested in Mr Hatcher's bridge scheme?"

"Bifrost? You think his death had something to do with that?"

"We're making no presumptions," said Sugarbrook. "We are in a uniquely tricky situation in that Mr Medawar was murdered aboard a bus containing only a limited number of people."

"You've spoken to those impersonator chaps, have you?"

Sugarbrook inclined his head. "My officers have interviewed the two actors."

"And so you assume that someone on board the bus had a motive to kill David?"

"Random motiveless murders are rare things."

"You hear stories about people just going bananas with a machete in crowded places and wotnot."

"Bananas with a machete," said Sugarbrook, an eyebrow raised. "Mental health issues can play a role in some incidents. I don't think that's what's happening here, do you?"

"Oh, don't ask me," said Bunty cheerfully. "I can't understand why people kill each other at all. It sounds like far too much effort and, frankly, not very nice."

"Motives tend to be limited. Usually it's base emotions or occasionally personal gain. It seems no one here really knew David well enough to either love him or hate him."

"So money, then?" said Bunty.

Sugarbrook consulted his papers. "Tell me about this Bifrost project."

Bunty smiled. "Ah. Yes. Wonderful concept. Tom's done all the donkey work. He had to bring all the investors together because he's totally strapped for cash, but really it was all my idea originally."

Diana remembered Stuart Dinktrout had said something similar.

"Was it?" asked Sugarbrook.

"Mmm. Tom and I shared a room in our first year at uni. Favourite game was 'damp tissue in the pot'."

"Mm-hmm?"

"Oh. On mornings after the night before when we'd had too many shandies we'd often not get out of bed. That's separate beds, by the way. Just to be clear. We'd challenge each other to lob little balls of wadded tissue into the tea pot on the desk. Oh, it sounds juvenile now that I say it and a damned waste of young, keen minds, but if you can't waste time playing silly buggers then what can you do?"

"Go on," said Sugarbrook.

"And I'd simply said one morning that wouldn't it be a fine thing if you could throw a tissue over and then, you know, get the teapot or a fresh cup of tea to come back. Silly, idle speculation but from such things, great ideas grow." He looked from Sugarbrook to Quigley as though hoping they'd understand. "To be clear, Bifrost is a massive bridge-building system. Nothing to do with damp tissue or pots of tea."

"I'd hope not," said Sugarbrook. "This whole project. How much has been invested in it?"

Bunty puffed out his cheeks. "From the initial circle of investors, I believe Tom has raised a little shy of two million pounds."

Sugarbrook cleared his throat.

"That's just the money to work on the prototype," Bunty continued. "Tom's signed the agreement with Tower Division Engineering. He should be meeting their top bod today, *if* you let him out in time." He leaned back, smiling. "And then it's full steam ahead. Manufacturing, military application and buns for tea for everyone."

"So, a lot of money at stake," said Sugarbrook.

A shrug. "If you like. But even if David didn't know many of us that well, that doesn't mean something wasn't going on."

"What do you mean?"

"There's always *something* going on... it's like the crying I heard."

"What crying?" said Sugarbrook.

"Well, I *thought* I heard crying. The night before old David bought the farm. Late at night, I heard this sob, almost immediately outside my hotel room. I was still awake. I heard and thought 'hello, that's a queer noise' and got up to look outside in case there was some poor girl there."

"And was there?" asked Sugarbrook.

"A poor girl? No. But I did see David and our Tom in the corridor talking. David looked quite angry and Tom was saying something like, 'not worth crying over though, is it?'"

"One of them had been crying?"

"Oh no, I don't think so," said Bunty. "Dry eyes, the pair of them. But David didn't seem best pleased, anyway."

Chapter Twenty-Nine

Zaf tracked down the hotel cleaner, Carmen, by following the sound of the vacuum cleaner. Once he'd brought her back to the function room and shown her the situation with the tablecloths, she nodded in understanding.

She flicked through the clean ones, counting. "Enough here for today, I think."

She loaded the dirty ones onto her trolley, and then balled up the ripped ones into a waste bag. "All good."

She went to push her trolley out of the room, but Zaf blocked her way. "Wait. No one will get punished for this, will they?"

Carmen shrugged. "For tablecloths? No. Nobody knows how many tablecloths there are. Only me."

She winked at him and headed off along the corridor. He returned to the function room, determined to keep the group's mood buoyant.

"Next activity!" he announced.

There were muted groans, but also some shuffling to attention.

"We spent some time on the fashion show," he said, "which I guess appealed more to some of you than others. Well, the tables are about to be turned, because our second activity will be building a bridge!"

The bridge group sat tall in their seats, looking like they might burst with excitement. The women of the hen party shrugged at each other.

"Let me explain the rules," said Zaf. "In a moment I'll set up the gorge your bridge will need to cross."

"Gorge?" said one of the hens.

"A gap between tables. Needless to say, the floor beneath the table is lava, and you can't support your bridge from below. Your bridge should be created mostly using the items I'm about to give you, but you can add other minor additions if you have them." He eyed the groups. "I want to make one thing very clear, though."

"What's that?" asked Arwen.

"No tablecloths are to be harmed in the building of this bridge."

She sniggered, then bit her lip.

Zaf delved into the bag at his feet and pulled out two packets that he held up.

"Right, here's your bridge building material. You've each got a pack of extra-long spaghetti. The gorge will be wider than this, so you'll need to get creative."

Zaf had persuaded one of the police officers to go and buy the spaghetti from the corner shop, while she was doing a run for crisps and snacks. He spent a few minutes creating a gorge for each team, making sure they were both the same size.

"Right teams, your time starts now. You have an hour and a half to design and build your bridge."

Tom's hand shot up. "Can we build more than one bridge?"

Zaf shook his head; he didn't want each bridge enthusiast building their own.

"Part of this challenge is for you to work together. One bridge per team, please. And I nearly forgot the most important thing. Your finished bridge needs to support the weight of an egg. I haven't got any eggs, which is probably best for the carpet, so we will use a salt shaker thingy instead. Is everyone clear on the rules?"

"Double or quits, boys," said Bethan. "Forty quid to the winning team!"

"Let's make this more interesting, shall we?" said Stuart. "I will offer a bottle of the finest wine that this hotel can provide to the winner. How about that?"

Bunty snorted as he emerged from the interview cupboard. "We all know that your idea of fine wine will be some Bordeaux, high in punch and low in class. I'll offer a decent Burgundy to the winner. You can use Stuart's as mouthwash or something."

There was chuckling from the bridge group and eager nods from the hens.

Zaf sat back and watched as the two groups huddled to discuss their designs.

"Some musical accompaniment while we work?" suggested Bunty. He fiddled with his phone and moments later the room's speakers were playing Frank Sinatra.

The bridge group had the advantage of knowing names and techniques. Their conversation had already moved onto into what they might use for ties.

Death at Tower Bridge   147

The hen party were on a steeper learning curve.

"How about we all take a couple of pieces of spaghetti and spend five minutes working on ideas?" said Arwen. "Then we all share our ideas with the group."

"OK." Bethan opened the packet and pulled out a handful of spaghetti, breaking it into small pieces as she did so.

"What on earth are you doing?" Lydia yelled. "The length of the spaghetti is crucial to this!"

"But I always break up spaghetti," said Bethan. "So it fits in the pan." She looked at the pieces in her hands, as if seeing them for the first time. "Oh, yeah. I shouldn't have done that." She looked up. "It's not *all* broken. Maybe we can get some more?"

She looked over to Zaf, who held up his hands. There was no more spaghetti.

"What kind of a person breaks up spaghetti to fit it into the pan, anyway?" asked Lydia. "You soften the ends and coil it round."

Bethan looked at her with suspicion. "Then one end would be more cooked than the other end."

"We're not here to swap recipes," said Lydia, "we're here to win a competition. Please try to get on board with what we're doing, will you?"

"Wait!" interrupted Gaynor. "I think Bethan's had an idea."

"She did?" said Lydia.

"I did?" said Bethan.

The bridge group were sketching designs and arguing furiously with each other.

"Tom," said Bunty, "I don't know whether it's completely escaped your notice, but in this particular challenge, we have a godlike ability to reach down from the sky and place our materials precisely where we need them, without any requirement for cranes or other solutions to the issue of access. Deployment is not our problem."

"I get you Bunty, but it's such a great opportunity to showcase Bifrost's star offering."

"Showcase it to whom?"

Tom waved his arms to encompass the room, but his gaze snagged on Zaf. Zaf smiled, pleased that Tom wanted to impress him.

Stuart leaned in. "Voice of reason here. Always happy to support someone with a vision, you know that, lad. You have a plan, do you? Some way that we can achieve what you're talking about with our limited resources?"

"A plan? I most certainly do. It'll need testing, of course." Tom sat back in his chair, looking pleased with himself.

"What do you say we indulge the young 'un? Give him twenty minutes to make a proof of concept."

"Fine," said Bunty. "Get on with it, Tom."

Tom leaned forward. "Right. I need you all to put every pen that you own onto the table. I need one that's retractable."

Bunty and Stuart exchanged glances and began to search their pockets.

Tom looked over at Zaf. "Got a retractable pen?"

Zaf searched his pockets and his bag. At any given time he carried four or five pens, and a pencil, too, in case of wet weather. He pulled out several before finding a retractable one.

"The clicky sort, yeah?"

"Perfect!" said Tom. "D'you mind if it gets destroyed in the name of science?"

Zaf laughed. "No. What d'you plan to use it for?"

"Come over and see." Tom patted the seat beside him.

Zaf sat down, close to Tom.

"So Bifrost's target customer is the military," said Tom, addressing the group but occasionally glancing sideways at Zaf. "Where there is a situation that calls for emergency bridge solutions, potentially in a hostile environment, that is where the Bolt-To-Bridge is needed."

"Bolt-To-Bridge?" asked Zaf.

"Yes, in the sense of a crossbow bolt. We send in an armoured truck that reverses into position." Tom used his mobile phone as the truck and manoeuvred it to the edge of the gorge. "Once it's lined up, it has twin mechanisms built onto the rear that will fire high-tensile wires attached to crossbow bolts, as anchoring points on the other side. Once we've confirmed that the anchoring is secure on both sides, the bridge will unfurl from the back of the truck and be hydraulically pushed to the other side. That gives us vehicular access to the other side in less than fifteen minutes."

"Wow." Zaf was impressed. He could see it in his mind, a James Bond truck that could rock up and make a bridge happen anywhere.

"Neat, isn't it?" Tom's eyes sparkled.

"It really is," said Zaf. "How d'you make sure the anchoring is secure on the other side, though?"

Tom's smile faltered. "There are a number of techniques. It depends on the terrain, obviously. There is a drone solution in development, but sometimes it's easiest to just send an operative across on the initial line."

That didn't sound entirely safe, but Zaf wasn't an expert. "Cool. So you're planning to use the retractable pens as teeny tiny crossbows?"

Tom nodded. "I want to see if the springs are strong enough, yeah. I think it could work."

"I can't wait to see it. I'll leave you to your testing and see how the other team's doing." Zaf stood up. "Oh, it seems you might be in demand."

He indicated the interview cupboard. Sugarbrook was pointing a chunky finger straight at Tom.

Chapter Thirty

Tom looked irritated as he entered the interview cupboard.

"I'm in the middle of important business out there."

Sugarbrook shook his head. "We are conducting a murder inquiry."

"Well, yes. Yes, of course." Tom sat next to Diana, having the decency to look sheepish. "Miss Bakewell," he said.

She gave him a nod in return.

"You spoke to David Medawar late on the Thursday night," the DCI said.

"Did I?"

"You were seen in the corridor around midnight."

Tom frowned. "Well, only for a moment or two. I'd just come out because I'd heard a noise."

"What noise?"

"Crying, I think."

"And so you went out and...?"

"David was there. Outside his room."

"He'd been crying?"

"No. I assumed at first that he'd come out because he'd heard it, but I think he was more the cause."

"What do you mean?"

"One of the girls was hurrying down the corridor. Hurrying away."

Sugarbrook gestured at the function room beyond this smaller space. "One of the women out there?"

Tom nodded, then frowned. "I told you this."

"You certainly did not."

"He'd been chatting with the women in the bar. The mother and the daughter. And it was the younger one—"

"Bethan."

"Exactly. The one with the arm. I saw her walking away as fast as she could."

DS Quigley was taking notes, her hand speeding across a notepad.

"And what did you surmise had happened before you came upon the scene?" asked Sugarbrook.

Tom drew back, a slight smirk on his face.

"Come on, now, Detective. I think you can work it out. A young woman from the valleys, come to the big city for a hen party, gets chatted up by some man in a suit that costs more than she makes in a month. Except I guess it didn't go quite as she would have liked."

"You think something untoward happened in David's room?"

A shrug. "People drink, people talk. Someone makes a move, someone doesn't like it. It had gone midnight. I hear tears come easy to some."

"Did David give you any details?"

"What am I, a gossip? I came out to see what had happened. David gave me the glibbest of stories."

"Bunty said he looked angry."

Tom considered. "He was. He'd been rebuffed, I guess. Frustrating and, like I said, it had gone midnight." He sniffed and looked at his watch. "Can I be frank?"

Sugarbrook tilted his head, saying nothing.

"I have a very important business meeting at five o'clock. Cat Garrett. The success of the Bifrost project pretty much hinges on that meeting. What's the chances of me getting out of here by then?"

"Again, this is a murder enquiry."

"Oh, I am fully aware."

Sugarbrook exhaled through his nose. To Diana, the man seemed to be a mass of pent-up emotion, like a sleeping volcano that might one day erupt.

"I have a few other questions," he said, "but I imagine you will be free to go soon enough."

"And I'll make sure you get there on time," added Diana.

Chapter Thirty-One

Zaf sat down with the hen party. Someone had fetched a kettle and a hairdryer from a bedroom. Pieces of spaghetti were soaking in mugs, and there was a small pile of mush that he was trying not to look at. It looked like someone had part-chewed a pile of spaghetti and spat it out.

"How's your bridge doing?" he asked.

Gaynor cradled something close to her chest as she leaned over the table. "I need more paste. Pass it over here! I'll smoosh the next section, Bethan you can dry it."

Gaynor slid a piece of paper across to Bethan, who was wielding the hairdryer. She blasted the paper with the full force of the hottest setting.

Zaf wanted to ask questions, but the noise made it impossible. He moved round to the other side.

"Lydia, can you tell me what you're making?"

Lydia had a cup of the soaked spaghetti chunks. She fished them out onto a small plate. "I'm on paste-creating duty. Gaynor's building and Bethan's drying."

"Uh-huh. So you're doing what, exactly?"

"We're using chewed-up pasta as glue to stick the dried stuff into beams. Then we'll stick the beams together to make a bridge."

Lydia popped the pasta into her mouth and started to chew, her face a grimace.

Zaf pulled back. He didn't fancy hanging around for the spitting-out part.

It was a peculiar approach, but it had simplicity on its side. A glance across at the bridge team suggested that a simple approach might just prove to be the winner.

Tom Hatcher came out of the interview cupboard and hurried to join his team.

"Miss Griffiths," DCI Sugarbrook called across the room.

Several heads turned.

"Bethan," he said, clarifying.

Bethan passed her hairdryer to another woman, Natalie, and went over to the cupboard.

Zaf checked the time.

"You're halfway through your time," he called out to the teams. "Forty-five minutes left."

He went over to see how the bridge team were getting on. Tom had thrust himself back into the fray.

"It's going to work," he said. "When we put all the springs together it will carry the cord."

He'd unthreaded a cord from a hoody, which he waved in his hand.

"It's time to build an actual bridge now," said Stuart. "Tom, if you want to keep on with your proof of concept then that's fine, but the rest of us need to move into construction or there's a danger we'll have nothing to show."

Tom made exasperated noises, but gave a dismissive

wave. "Go on without me. I'll get this prototype working, it might earn us some extra brownie points with the judge. Coolness points." He winked at Zaf.

Bunty plonked himself down by the gorge, his fist full of spaghetti. "Excellent. We need ties."

"I have spent a fruitful half an hour unravelling the fine wool of my cravat," said Stuart, "so I have plenty of thread."

"We're in business," said Bunty. "Although I am really not sure that it's a cravat if it's made from wool."

"It's a cravat if I style it as a cravat," Stuart replied, making a twiddly flourish at his neckline by way of demonstration.

"Fair enough. Let's build ourselves a gorgeous little truss bridge, shall we?"

Zaf strolled around the room, trying not to pay too much attention to the details of the two team's methods. Partly so the results would be a surprise, and partly to avoid the sight of Lydia spitting out pasta.

Chapter Thirty-Two

Bethan blinked at DCI Sugarbrook, taking in the question he'd just asked her.

Diana placed her hand over Bethan's and squeezed it. She tried to read Bethan's reaction: caught in headlights, yes. But was there a hint there of caught doing something she shouldn't be doing, too?

"It's a simple enough question," said Sugarbrook. "Were you with David Medawar on Thursday night? Not in the bar, but up in his room."

A pink blotchiness had broken out on Bethan's face and her breaths were shallow.

"You have to promise you won't tell my mum. She'll get the wrong end of the stick."

"Wrong end of the stick about what?"

"I was there," Bethan said, licking her lips. "I'd gone to speak to him. It's true."

"So when you' said you'd only met him in the bar, that was a lie."

"I wasn't... lying. It just wasn't relevant. It..."

"Yes?"

She pulled on a smile. "David had had my mum talking to him all evening. If he wasn't an expert on Hodgkin Lymphoma before we met him, he certainly was after. I could tell he understood."

"Understood what?"

"It can be draining looking after someone. D'you know how many hospital appointments I've taken my mum to? I've lost count. The amount of tricky conversations I've had to have at work. The jewellery company's really small. There's only eight of us. Me taking days off affects everyone. And they've been lovely, of course, but... It's been a burden." She closed her eyes and shook her head. "Mum is *not* a burden. I love her. But that doesn't mean it's not hard."

Tears trickled down her cheeks. Diana produced a tissue and Bethan dabbed her face.

"Your sister helps out?" suggested Sugarbrook.

Bethan's laugh was sharp and bitter. "From three hundred miles away in London? No. There's me. Only me. Always has been. And that lovely David feller had seen what it was like, just chatting with me and Mum for a bit and, yeah, I did go to his room and we just talked some more. I just let it all out."

"There was nothing... romantic in what occurred between you?"

Another laugh. "Like I have time for that. No. And I don't think he was interested in me that way." She looked up with a shrug. "Maybe he was. Maybe I was too wrapped up in my own problems to see it. But he was kind and he listened. But please don't tell my mum."

"Why not?"

"Because she'll jump to the same conclusions you have.

My mum's lovely but she thinks she needs to look out for me all the while, protect me from predatory men."

"Does she think there are predatory men in your life?"

"She thinks all men are like that." Bethan wiped the last of the tears away, her composure recovered. "Arwen was only able to get herself a man because she did it so far from home."

"That must feel... restrictive," said the DCI.

Bethan looked down at her hands, clutched together in her lap.

"Mum's not got long left. The wedding, this trip. We're enjoying life together while we can and maybe my life will begin when this is all over. But I'm in no hurry for that to happen."

Sugarbrook nodded slowly. "Your meeting with David Medawar, late that night, was helpful."

"It was."

"Friends said he looked angry."

"What friends?"

"He was seen in the corridor. They said he looked angry."

"It'd be that difficult conversation."

"You mentioned that before. What exactly did he say?"

Bethan shook her head. "I don't remember. But he'd been... betrayed, I think. Someone had let him down. He didn't care for bridges and stuff. That was clear. But he needed to confront someone."

"Who?"

"I've got no idea."

Chapter Thirty-Three

Zaf called a loud, slow countdown, and announced that the two bridge-building teams were out of time.

"Tools down everyone, that's it! Time for the judging. Let's switch the order and start with the bridge group. Gents, can you show us what you've done?"

Tom stood first. "As you know, I wanted to wow you all with a live action deployment, powered by pen springs."

"You wanted to catapult a bridge over the chasm."

"In true Bifrost style. But since I spent half the time talking to the police, it's no surprise I couldn't get that working, so the task of actually building a bridge fell to my colleagues here."

Stuart stood with a huff. "Yes, well. A valuable lesson about teamworking has perhaps been learned in this corner. Did we have a decent design for a bridge? Yes, we did. Bunty, would you show everyone our pencil sketch?"

Bunty held up a picture of something that looked like a scaffolding tower on its side.

"We'd planned to build a truss bridge," he said, "made up

of nice strong triangles. The design depends upon a lot of joins. In an ideal world we would have blobs of blu-tac, or perhaps marshmallows to use as ties at those junctions, but we did not have those things. We decided to tie the joints, with yarn that Stuart harvested from a scarf."

"Cravat," said Stuart.

"It's a scarf, Stuart. Anyway, it died an honourable death to donate its yarn to the project. Let's have a moment's silence for Stuart's scarf."

Bunty doffed an imaginary hat and stood to attention for a long moment.

"So," he continued. "The part where it all fell down was actually making the ties work. Maybe someone with more nimble fingers could have succeeded, but all I can report is that we broke a lot of spaghetti, and sent a fair bit of it flying through the air."

Zaf clapped lightly as Bunty sat down. "Thank you for an entertaining and enlightening narrative. Am I to take it that you have no bridge to demonstrate?"

"That is correct," grunted Bunty.

The Bridget Jones fans clapped politely and Zaf noticed some glances between them. With their opponents out of the game, did they smell a potential victory?

"Let's look at our other group, then," he said. "Ladies, would you like to show us what you've got?"

Arwen stood and coughed. "Well, we're not as technical as the other group, so we improvised. We have got a working bridge though, which I'm gonna demonstrate. Pass me the salt cellar please, Lydia."

She stood with her hands wide, presenting the bridge to the room. Lydia nipped round and photographed her, then passed the salt cellar.

"So the inspiration for this construction came from Bethan," said Arwen, "who broke up a load of spaghetti for cooking. We had a chat and thought we could use cooked spaghetti as glue."

There were sounds of scoffing from the bridge group. "Surely not," said Bunty. "It'll never hold."

"So we cooked it," said Arwen, "and carefully, um, ground it into a paste. Then we used it to make slabs from pieces of spaghetti and dried them with a hairdryer. Once we had enough slabs, we overlapped and glued those together to make our bridge."

"Well I never," said Tom. "They made a clapper bridge."

Zaf had no idea what a clapper bridge was, but he was impressed. The bridge resembled the crusty mess that sometimes formed in the bottom of his bin, but it was a bridge.

"So here's our bridge," said Arwen, "and now we'll perform the salt cellar test."

She settled the salt cellar onto the centre of the bridge, as gently as she could.

The whole room was silent as they waited to see if it would break under the weight. After a pause of several seconds, Zaf clapped hard. "I think we have a winner!"

The applause from both groups was genuine and enthusiastic. The hen party were relieved that their bridge had survived, and the bridge group clearly had grudging admiration for the unusual low-tech methods.

"Let's not forget how very entertaining our bridge group was in sacrificing Stuart's scarf," said Zaf. "They get a bonus point for that. But our overall winners for today's activities are the hens. Well done everyone!"

"So does this mean we get those two bottles of wine?" asked Arwen.

Zaf turned to Stuart and Bunty.

Stuart stood and bowed deeply. "You earned them with your ingenuity. We'll go and sort that out now. Come on, Bunty."

"And I'd best go deal with our pile of tablecloths," said Zaf.

The police officer at the door held up a hand as Stuart and Bunty made to leave. "We all need to stay here, Sirs."

"That's OK," said Sugarbrook, coming out of the cupboard with Bethan Griffiths. "I think we're all done for today. In fact, I think we're done, full stop."

He stepped forward to address the guests. "I would like to thank you all for your patience. We might need to talk to some of you again over the coming days but for now you are free to go."

"Free at last!" declared one of the men, fists raised.

"The tour's back on?" said one of the women.

"Tomorrow," said Diana. "Chartwell and Crouch will ensure your Sunday is jam-packed with fun and activity."

"We get our bridges?" asked Stuart with a raised eyebrow.

Diana smiled. "Bridges and Bridget all day long."

Tom was throwing on his jacket. "I must get to my meeting. If I can make it in time."

"We promised we would get you there," Diana said. "Where is it?

"Tower Division Engineering, Marsh Wall in Canary Wharf."

"The quickest route will be a tube to Canary Wharf."

"And then walk from there," added Zaf.

"If you'd show me," Tom said.

Zaf realised Tom was looking at him. He glanced at Diana, who nodded.

"Let's get our skates on, then," he said.

"Want any of us to come?" asked Stuart.

"This is nothing more than a formality," said Tom.

"Besides, someone owes us a bottle of wine and forty quid," said Bethan.

"Then it sounds like we should all retire to the bar. First drink's on Chartwell and Crouch," said Diana.

Zaf gave Diana a look, then hurried from the room behind Tom.

Chapter Thirty-Four

The tour group had spent almost the entire day cooped up together in the function room, and many were relieved to be able to return to their rooms or go outside and stretch their legs. True to his word, Stuart Dinktrout bought a bottle of white for the women, a very reasonable Chateauneuf-du-Pape in Diana's opinion.

A couple of the men said they'd like to get a breath of fresh air before the evening meal. Diana stepped out onto Chiltern Street with them to suggest a direction they could walk in.

"221b Baker Street is up that way," she said. "If you're interested in the homes of fictional detectives. There's a statue of Sherlock Holmes there, too."

The men thanked her and set off. Diana turned to see Gaynor Griffiths, mother of the bride, sitting on a bench in the Redhouse Hotel's front courtyard garden.

Gaynor's pallor was only exacerbated by her vibrant wig.

"You OK?" Diana asked.

"Just needed some space. A bit of quiet." Gaynor looked

back at the hotel. "Oh, I love time with the girls. I treasure every moment." She took a deep breath. "Do you worry about the people around you?"

"Constantly."

"I spend my life worrying about others. I worry that Arwen is rushing headlong into big decisions. I worry that Bethan is putting her life on hold for me and missing out."

"Do they have a father? Do you have a husband or partner?"

Gaynor shook her head. "We separated over twenty years ago. He moved to Australia. No interest in seeing the girls, he's not even coming to Arwen's wedding."

"I'm sorry to hear that."

"I'm not." Gaynor laughed. "He travelled for work way back when, and I realised I was happiest when he wasn't there. And so was he. The moment we admitted that to each other, things got a lot better." She took a deep breath. "Sometimes I think I'm at my best when I'm alone. Me and my illness. I cope better with the pain, the tiredness." She placed her hands on her knees. "Sometimes, and this might sound silly, but it feels like we only see the bad things in life when someone else is watching."

"I'm not sure I follow," Diana said.

"It's like an untidy house. It only really bothers you if you've got guests."

"Ah, I see."

"When I'm alone, I can cope." She closed her eyes and took another deep breath. "Just me and the universe. Being at one with things." She opened one eye to look at Diana. "It's a bit late in the game for me to become a Buddhist monk, isn't it?"

"Oh, I don't know." Diana smiled.

"I've got the hair for it, obviously." Gaynor laughed enough that Diana felt comfortable joining in.

"When my Bethan was laid up with her broken arm for a fortnight and Arwen was wrapped up in her wedding plans and, to be blunt, the pair of them left me alone, I felt better than I had in months. Does that make me ungrateful?"

"It means you're honest."

"Honest. Yes, I am. I should put that in my diary." Gaynor cast about herself and then remembered the lost diary. She wagged her finger down the road. "Sherlock Holmes didn't really live down there, did he?"

"No, he was an entirely fictional detective," said Diana. She had to explain that so often to tourists that it was no longer a surprise.

"Ah." Gaynor wrinkled her nose. "Thought it was a load of nonsense. How much the ash had melted in the butter and what colour mud someone had on their shoes. I'm sure the writer made it up as he went along."

"Arthur Conan Doyle? Possibly. In the days before the internet it was possibly easier to invent things. He had medical training though, and brought much of that knowledge to his work."

"I suppose."

"I'm reading an Agatha Christie novel at the moment," Diana said. "Actually, I read one last night and I started another this morning over breakfast. She had a background in the sciences too, and included a lot of that in her work."

"Someone told me there have been real-life crimes solved because the police recognised similarities with Agatha Christie's books."

"Really?" Diana said. She wasn't sure if she was impressed by this, or thought it was nonsense.

"Yep. Life is strange."

Diana took a breath. "Bethan's broken arm. She said she ran into a lamppost."

Gaynor grunted. "I was with her in A and E. What do they call it? A spiral fracture or something. Someone took hold of my girl's arm and twisted. Turned it right round until it snapped." Her face hardened. "A bloke did that to her. She doesn't make the right choices in life."

"No?"

"She's got what they call an addictive personality. She doesn't know when to back away. She can't see the warning signs. Can't see when to stop."

Diana gave the woman a supportive smile, unsure what to say. "Will you be coming in soon to join the others?"

A nod. "Give me a few more moments alone with the universe, love."

Diana went inside.

The hotel lobby was empty, no guests and no staff. But Diana could hear raised voices from the office behind reception.

"As if yesterday's fiasco wasn't enough!" a man was saying. "We'll be lucky if that wedding party don't sue. It's a simple matter of getting the right things to the right place, Penny. It should be well within the capabilities of a competent receptionist."

"I agree," said a female voice: Penny, Diana realised. "And you know I always check and double—"

"I've had it up to here with excuses. This business with the music system being hacked is the last straw. The wedding having the wrong music is one thing, but having *New York, New York* blasting out at the wake today is intolerable."

"It was a Bluetooth issue. Someone in the room next door had connected to it."

"Oh, you mean your group of wanted criminals?"

"I was trying to accommodate our guests—"

"And half the London Met?"

"Chartwell and Crouch always use our hotel. I was trying to assist and—"

"Trying, trying, trying. I don't care if the bloody fools the Met were interviewing hacked the speaker system—"

"Hardly hacked, Mr Lezar."

"But it happened on your watch, and there's no excusing it."

"Look, I need a few days anyway. I've had a text from my grandma. She's not well."

"Oh, I'll give you more than a few days, Penny. Here."

Diana stood there, knowing she should move away but rooted to the spot. Eventually, Penny Slipper emerged from the door behind the counter. She carried a cardboard box and was on the verge of tears.

Diana stepped forward. "You've lost your job?"

Penny tried to smile. "I need to go, Diana. I hope…"

She bowed her head and hurried out to the street.

Diana ran to catch up.

"This was our fault," she said.

"Oh, it's a lot of things," said Penny, striding down Chiltern Street. "And he was right to fire me."

"Nonsense!" Diana replied. "You're the best shepherd of guests I've ever known."

Penny barked out a laugh. "Carlton Lezar didn't think so. Too many hiccups on my watch. It's my job to figure out what's about to go wrong and prevent that."

"You can't be psychic."

"A good receptionist is."

They were both still walking, but now Penny had slowed enough to allow Diana to catch up.

"I'll find something else eventually," said Penny. "Don't worry about me."

Diana gestured towards the bus depot, ahead of them. "You could work for us. The tour business needs people with your skills."

"After the amount of times I've heard you complaining about your manager?"

"Managerially we are at a low point," Diana conceded. "But things change."

Gus was sitting on the pavement outside the depot garage, licking his paw to clean his ears.

"We had a great manager in Morris Walker," Diana said. "He, not unlike you, paid the price for other people's mistakes. But even if we have to put up with Paul Kensington for now, we'll claw our way back up."

Penny bent down to tickle the top of Gus's head. The cat responded by arching his back and purring.

"I'm sure you will," she said. "Tomorrow I'll be heading home to sort out some family matters. But right now, I just want to stomp off into the sunset."

Diana smiled. "I can't fault that. But if you're prepared to stomp in the direction of my favourite café, then I can buy a cup of tea and a slice of cake."

Penny stood up.

"Things might look better after a cup of tea and a slice of cake," said Diana.

Penny smiled. "Maybe."

Chapter Thirty-Five

"Up this way," said Zaf, taking the stairs up from Canary Wharf tube station.

"Right-o," said Tom, following closely behind.

At street level, Zaf swiftly oriented himself and turned in the direction they needed to walk.

"For a Brummie, you seem to know London really well."

"I'm a quick learner," Zaf told him, setting off across Jubilee Park to Bank Street. "I've been swotting up on my Tower Bridge facts for tomorrow's trip."

"Is that so?" Tom grinned. "Let's start with its height then."

"Pardon?"

"How tall is it?"

"Sixty-five metres."

"I'll check that later, obviously. Next question then, how many times a year does the bridge open for river traffic?"

"Around a thousand. Boom!" Zaf punched the air.

"Last question, then, what is the number of the road that crosses over on the bridge?"

Zaf opened and closed his mouth. "It's the Tower Bridge Road," he said, knowing he wasn't answering the question. "The ring road."

Tom pulled a sad face. "Sorry contestant, the answer was the A100."

"I knew that!" Zaf said.

"Oh, really?"

"I did. I should have had more faith in myself."

Tom's eyes lingered on Zaf's face.

"You seem a confident enough guy as it is. So, I take it that you came to London to experience a bit more of life?"

"Perhaps."

"Get away from the parochial attitudes of the folk up north."

Zaf laughed. "Birmingham isn't in the north. Far from it. And parochial? You do know Birmingham is the second biggest city after London? Over a million people."

Tom gave him a frown. "Really? Surely Manchester's the second biggest."

"Pah. Manchester doesn't even make the top five. Down here." He turned a corner, letting Tom follow. "Birmingham is big and bustling and welcoming but London... ah, there's something about London that no other city can match."

"True." Tom stopped in front of an office block with various company names on a plate, including that of Tower Division Engineering. "Anyway, this is me. Maybe after I've gone in and signed a few documents with Cat and sorted things out, you and I could meet up for a drink to celebrate my success. And you can show me this city of yours."

A tingle ran up Zaf's spine. "I could definitely do that."

"Cool." Tom looked at him with a *time-for-you-to-leave* look. Zaf couldn't blame him; who'd want a tour guide hanging around a business meeting?

He gave Tom a grin then turned back for the tube. He took the Jubilee Line back to Green Park then changed for the Victoria Line to Pimlico and home to Eccleston Square.

As he approached the house, Alexsei was emerging with a big cardboard box in his hands.

"Ah," he said. "How often it is I see you coming back home before Diana?"

Zaf narrowed his eyes. It wasn't Alexsei's business to police his working hours.

"We're both done for the day," he said, checking his phone. "She says she's had to stay out for *emergency tea and cake*, whatever that means."

"I see." Alexsei juggled the box in his hands. "Items for the birthday barbecue tomorrow evening. You will be coming?"

The suggestion that Zaf wouldn't come irritated him even more.

"Coming? I'll be bringing the party!"

Alexsei frowned. "How so?"

"I mean... I mean it'll be fun because I'm there." Was he sounding silly?

"Of course," Alexsei said. "Many people will be there. I hope they will all be enjoying themselves."

Zaf thought back to the entry in Diana's diary.

"Do you know anyone called Pascal?" he asked.

"Who?"

"I think it might have been a boyfriend from back in the day."

"Diana knows lots of people." Alexsei shrugged and

jiggled his box again. "I must take this." He walked past Zaf, paused and turned back. "Do you think I do not like you?"

"What?"

"You think I am 'off' with you?"

"Were you listening in?"

Alexsei ignored the question. "I think you think I think you're a fool."

"I... I..." Zaf struggled to untie the sentence. But yes, he did think Alexsei saw him as a fool.

"I don't think you're a fool," Alexsei said. "There is something foolish about you, yes. Your manner is gawkish and naïve. And you seem to make the most terrible noise when you come home late. And you do seem to always act without thinking of the consequences of your actions."

Zaf watched Alexsei. Was there going to be a 'but', after which Alexsei would reel off Zaf's more positive qualities?

No. Alexsei smiled and left with his box.

Zaf watched him head for the garden, then trudged upstairs.

He had time alone before Diana returned, which made him think of the diary in her room.

Would it be bad to go and have another peek?

Of course it would.

But this time, he had an excuse for his snooping. The mysterious Pascal from Diana's diary might just come to her birthday party. And he, Zaf, could engineer a touching reunion.

Diana clearly wasn't having a good day: the *emergency tea and cake* told him that much. Bringing together a couple of people who were destined to be together would be just what the doctor ordered.

Chapter Thirty-Six

Zaf crept into Diana's room and looked at the bookshelf.

Should he browse the 2000 diary, or try another?

He pulled out 2001 and flicked through some entries, looking for another mention of Pascal.

"Ooh yes!"

Took a trip to The Epicurean in Covent Garden with Pascal. I know what he wants from me now and I'm happy to oblige. We reminisced about how London's restaurant scene has changed and the rise of celebrity chefs.

I had the coq au vin. Pascal chose a pork casserole thing with a posh name I can't remember. I'd be useless at Pascal's job. Sometimes I need him as much as he needs me.

Crème brûlée dessert and a sticky pudding wine that I hated for reasons I struggled to put into words. Tonight's adventure could be in the papers at the weekend. Ariadne has moved out. I think everyone is happier for that. We can all move on with our lives.

What with his discovery of Diana's role as a backing singer on a top ten hit, this was shaping up to be quite the romantic soap opera. Diana and Ariadne, backing singers together, one ending up with the man who was clearly Mr Right for the other. Had they been so famous that their relationship turmoil was newsworthy? And how were Diana and Pascal not together now?

Zaf scanned more pages, hoping to find another mention, but was interrupted from a sound somewhere in the flat.

He put the diary down. Could Diana be back already?

He slammed the book back into place and ran from the room, then slowed to a casual saunter and tried not to look suspicious when he came across Diana in the hallway.

"Everything alright?" she asked, slipping off her jacket.

Zaf blew out his cheeks. "Of course. Why wouldn't it be?"

Diana nodded, her expression watchful.

"And you needed tea and cake?" he said.

She sighed, then then told him a sorry little story that ended with Penny Slipper getting fired from her job at the Redhouse Hotel.

"Poor Penny," Zaf said.

Diana looked at him. "I think by the end of it she seemed relieved."

"Relieved to be fired?"

"Freedom, even unwanted freedom, can be exhilarating. Anyway, I think she has a poorly relative in – Suffolk, isn't it?

– who she needs to visit. It seems our little group did cause her some headaches."

Zaf sagged.

"You do know that it's not your fault, don't you?" Diana said. "You did your very best with the group. They were bored and they did something that none of us imagined would be an issue."

But Zaf felt bad about the mess he'd created, even if it wasn't his fault. He really needed a win. Tracking down old flame Pascal and getting him to come to the barbecue could be that win.

"I think I might pop out for a walk," he said.

"Not been on your feet enough today?"

He wasn't about to tell her he was planning to track down a Holland Park house with a horseshoe over the door.

"I'm meeting a bloke for a drink," he said.

She smiled. "Tom Hatcher."

"Wh... How?"

"I don't think he could keep his eyes off you all day."

Zaf shook his head. "You've got eyes like a hawk."

"Ears of a rabbit, too. If you're coming in late, don't do that thing where you pretend to creep silently through the flat like a cat burglar. It never works."

"Understood."

Chapter Thirty Seven

Diana eyed Zaf over breakfast, marvelling at the fact he wasn't more tired. He'd come in after two last night, attempting to sneak around the flat despite her suggestion that he shouldn't. She'd tried to question him about his evening with Tom Hatcher, but all he'd wanted to talk about was a pub called The Castle with a beautiful tiled exterior.

Diana smiled. "The one on Holland Park Avenue."

Zaf frowned. "Was it? I'm not sure." He looked down, smiling to himself. "It was a good evening, though."

"I'm glad to hear it." She poured a second cup of tea from the pot.

He reached behind him and pulled an envelope out of his bag, which had been sitting on the floor by the door.

"Happy birthday."

Diana opened the card; a retro-styled image of Piccadilly Circus. She approved. "Thank you."

"I was going to bake you something for your birthday but I've been busy."

"I've noticed. Party's not until this evening. There may still be time."

He nodded.

"Shall we get the bus together?" she asked.

"Let's."

They made their way to the Redhouse Hotel in silence, Zaf occasionally rubbing his eyes. Perhaps he'd been more affected by his late night than she thought. That smile was still there, though.

His smile faded the moment they entered the Redhouse Hotel.

There was a new person on reception. He was tall and thin, wearing a huge, wary smile. Diana could tell he was from a temping agency.

Zaf sighed. It made Diana want to hug him.

"Can I be of assistance?" asked the receptionist.

"We're the tour guides from Chartwell and Crouch," Diana said. "We're collecting our guests."

"Ah. Yes." He consulted a piece of paper below the counter. "You're not to leave the lobby."

"Pardon?"

The man consulted the piece of paper again. "That's all it says. You're taking the guests off site but you 'must not' go into any other part of the hotel."

Diana didn't know whether to fume or to smile. The poor man had been given instructions by the manager, Mr Lezar, clearly keen to avoid any more upsets.

"We will stay here and wait," she said.

She watched Zaf stray towards the corridor that ran to the restaurant and the lifts. The receptionist tried not to look like he was staring at Zaf as he did.

Zaf stopped at the invisible borderline that would have

marked the beginning of the corridor, if there had been such an obvious thing as a 'beginning'. He wobbled between lobby and not-lobby. The poor temp's Adam's apple seemed to bob up in down in time to Zaf's naughty wobbling.

The tour group drifted out of the restaurant with an excited buzz of chatter. Diana kept one eye on Zaf and Tom Hatcher, but Zaf was being his most formally professional.

"We're going to take our tour of Tower Bridge this morning," he said, not meeting the eye of any group member.

"About bloody time," said Stuart Dinktrout.

"After that we'll stop at the diary shop from the Bridget Jones film," Diana said, "in case you need to purchase any luxury stationery items. Finally today we'll be visiting a wine bar local to Bridget's flat in Borough, before a mid-afternoon finish."

One of the women gave a lusty hurrah and several people, men and women, joined in.

"I understand that they have Bridget Jones themed cocktails for sale," Diana continued. "Today's itinerary has something for you all, I hope. Let's make the best of it."

On the way out to the bus, Lydia stopped to ask Diana a question. "Are the lookalikes coming back?"

Diana shook her head. "I'm so sorry. They were booked for a particular session."

"We didn't get as many pictures with them as we'd have liked."

"I am so sorry our tour was disrupted." Diana resisted adding *by a murder*.

Lydia sighed and boarded the bus. Newton had brought one of the closed-top buses today, possibly out of concern for the group members' sensibilities, but knowing Newton, possibly for some other reason entirely.

They took the scenic ride to Tower Bridge, past Hyde Park, St James's Park, and along the north bank of the Thames. Diana addressed the group as they crossed Tower Bridge. Did she find herself subconsciously filling the time they crossed with chatter, to block out memories of the last time they'd passed over here?

"Newton will park the bus on Tooley Street on the south side of the river, so we get the chance to admire the bridge from the bus once more. Then it's just a short walk to begin our tour."

The sun was shining and London was looking its very best.

"Tower Bridge famously stops traffic and lifts the road when a large vessel needs to pass through on the river."

Zaf held a hand out for the microphone. She passed it over.

"The arms of the bridge that lift up are the *bascules*. We wanted our bridge fans here to know that we tour guides are as willing to learn information as we are to impart it."

He handed the microphone back.

Diana smiled, wondering when Zaf had learned that fact and glad to see him animated again.

"There is a schedule online," she said. "I am pleased to say there is a bridge lift set for fifteen minutes' time, to allow the sailing barge Petal to proceed upriver. We should be able to see that."

An excited buzz erupted and the group filed off the bus and approached the bridge.

Diana made use of her distinctive duck head umbrella, holding it high to shepherd them down onto a grassed area with the best view.

She realised that Gaynor was falling behind. The walk

had only been a few hundred yards but was clearly a challenge for her.

"Here." Diana indicated a free bench for Gaynor to sit down while the rest of her family arranged themselves for photo opportunities. Bethan handed Gaynor her energy drink.

Stuart Dinktrout produced a camera bag with a selection of lenses. His bridge colleagues were torn between admiring the bridge and advising on lenses and camera settings.

"Here she comes!" called Zaf. The traffic lights had stopped the road traffic and the large boat was approaching, its ruddy masts in contrast to its bright white hull. Even though it was a sailing barge, it would be using its motors to pass along the Thames.

"Bascules up!" shouted Stuart as he snapped away.

Diana admired the sight; she never tired of watching the great bridge open.

"That's just lovely!" said Gaynor from her bench. "Thank you so much for organising this."

Diana smiled. All she'd done was keep an eye on the schedule.

Arwen and Lydia framed themselves with the bridge in the background, chatting to the phone as they recorded a video.

Tom tapped Zaf on the arm. "We do get to see the engine room on the tour, don't we?"

"Don't worry, you'll see everything."

Once the barge was through and the bridge was closed, the group went up to get themselves checked in for the tour.

Diana and Zaf gathered them together. "You may wish to make your own way through here. We will be going up this side of the bridge and then over the walkway to the other side. It's quite a few steps, but there are things to look at on the way up, so it shouldn't feel too arduous."

A hand shot up: Tom.

"I should mention that the engine room is accessed separately," said Diana, "through the same entrance as the gift shop. We will go there afterwards."

Tom's hand dropped.

"Is the walkway floor really glass?" Bethan asked.

"Only in parts," said Diana, "You can avoid it if you prefer." She turned to Gaynor. "Do you want to sit this one out?"

Gaynor shook her head. "I'll take it steady. Don't want to miss anything."

Chapter Thirty-Eight

They started up the stairs that ran through the northern tower. Diana led the way, Arwen close behind.

"Gotta get my steps in," she told Diana.

Diana glanced backwards. "I think some other members of your party might have to take it at slower pace."

"And they can. It's important to give people their space, isn't it?"

Diana resisted pointing out that moving a hundred and fifty miles away from your family was definitely 'giving them their space'.

"Do you think you'll ever have to go back to care for your mum?" she asked.

Arwen shook her head. "I don't know if she's as ill as she sometimes makes out."

"Oh?"

"Well, they've not called her in for any treatments in weeks and weeks."

"But she's still very ill," Diana persisted. Perhaps Gaynor was past the point where interventions were worth pursuing.

"I've not seen any all-clear letters, but she's had some really good weeks. It's not all downhill and..." Arwen looked back down the stairs. "They feed into each other."

"Who do?"

"Mum. Bethan. Living in each other's pockets. Mum leans too much on Bethan. Bethan fusses over Mum too much. You can be too close to someone. Emotionally, physically." She swallowed. "What's Bethan got? A full-time job breathing in noxious fumes."

"She works in jewellery design."

"Have you seen some of the materials they use? It's industrial, Diana. Then she's at home either fussing over Mum or staring mindlessly at her phone."

"You're on your phone a lot, too."

Arwen gave her a look. "I use mine mindfully. I'm building an online presence. Online poker and slot machines is not the same thing." She glanced back again. "Oh, they seem happy enough, but it's not healthy. Trust me."

Diana paused at the next landing to encourage the others on their way up, and took advantage of the opportunity to catch her breath.

"This very much reminds me of an old-fashioned railway station," said Stuart, coming up. "These girders painted over in the old brown and magnolia, whether it needs it or not. Look at the rivets! Hundred years of paint on every single one."

Diana nodded. The stairs were lined with pictures and posters. Tower Bridge had a treasure trail for younger visitors and there were drawings of a cartoon cat who looked a little like Gus.

"Check the Pale Horse. Cat at Tower not in diary," she said to herself.

"You alright?" asked Zaf, bringing up the rear with Gaynor.

"Oh, I'm fine," Diana told him.

"I wondered if oxygen starvation was making you talk gibberish."

Diana frowned. "It was written on the bookmark. Well, on the piece of hotel stationery he was using as a bookmark."

"Who?"

"David Medawar. *Check the Pale Horse. Cat at Tower not in diary.*"

Zaf pointed at the cartoon Tower Bridge cat. "Cat at Tower?"

"That's what I was thinking."

"The Pale Horse sounds like a pub," said Gaynor. "Or maybe that's because I'm thinking of pale ale."

"It's a Bible reference, isn't it?" said Zaf.

"Is it?" said Gaynor.

"*And I saw a rider on a pale horse and his name was Death.* Something like that."

Diana raised her eyebrows in surprise. "Full of information, our Zaf."

"I showed that David my diary," said Gaynor. "Because he was interested."

"Really?" Diana asked.

"Oh, it's not like Bridget Jones' diary. It's not all booze and fags and hanky-panky. I just kept a record of my illness in it. But I also used it as a gratitude journal. It's good for the soul. No cats, towers or horses in there, though."

They made their way to the top level. There was a large

display area with videos and exhibits. Beyond that was the walkway across to the other side.

Diana positioned herself to watch the expressions of the group as they stepped out and were faced with the breathtaking views over London. It was rewarding to see even the most cynical tourist struck with childlike wonder at the sight, and nobody disappointed.

"This is lush!" said Arwen. "We can see everything from up here." She bustled her hens into position for a group shot and asked Zaf to take their picture.

"I bet it was windy in the olden days," said Gaynor, who'd been paying attention to the displays. "No windows, just a railing, imagine!"

The hen party were absorbed by the views, while the men of the bridge party gravitated to any kind of display board, especially the ones with facts, figures and statistics.

"Can I take a group photograph of you?" Zaf asked the bridge group.

Most of them looked at each other as if he'd suggested something strange and alien, but Tom stepped forward and offered Zaf his phone.

"That would be wonderful."

The group shuffled together and posed, smiling only when Zaf demanded it.

Eventually the group descended on the south side of the bridge.

"Stick with them when we get outside," Diana whispered to Zaf. "We're likely to lose a few if we're not vigilant."

The walk to the gift shop and the engine room was a short one, but the bridge was so busy that Diana could see Zaf nipping hither and thither like a border collie nudging dawdling sheep back into the flock.

"Follow the blue line!" he called.

Predictably, the bridge group were enchanted by the engine room with its huge Victorian machinery. The hen party were more interested in the gift shop.

"Look!" said Zaf to Diana, holding up a souvenir mug featuring the Tower Bridge cat. "Their cat looks like Gus."

Gaynor had a basket full of small gifts. "I must take some bits for everyone!"

"Mum," groaned Arwen, "save yourself for the fancy diary shop."

"Plenty of room in here for these." Gaynor patting her handbag – Diana's handbag.

Diana smiled and said nothing.

Chapter Thirty-Nine

Once they had finished at Tower Bridge, Zaf led the group to meet Newton, who'd brought the bus back. Diana brought up the rear, keeping an eye on the mother of the bride.

Newton took them back across the bridge again as Zaf picked up the microphone.

"Now we're heading into the heart of the City of London. This is the part of London that gets to have special fancy bollards with stars and crests on. Look out for them! It's also where we will find the diary shop on Cornhill where, in the Bridget Jones movie, Bridget runs to find her true love, Mark Darcy."

"This is a long way from her flat, isn't it?" asked one of the women, Natalie.

"Yes," Zaf agreed. "I think they used on-screen trickery to make it seem closer, given that Bridget's flat in Borough's a full mile away and she runs here in her knickers."

"I have to say, I've never seen this bally film they're on

about," Bunty said to the man next to him, "but it sounds a hoot."

"Anyway, the building we'll be seeing is a grand old place," Zaf continued. "You can buy a diary if you feel like channelling your inner Bridget."

Newton dropped them off in Cornhill and the hen party were quick to find the shop on the corner featured in the film.

"Knickers!" shouted Arwen.

Zaf looked around to see she had her huge bag with her again. She rummaged through it and pulled out a handful of racy underwear.

"Um, what's going on?" asked Diana.

The women gathered round and pulled the knickers on over their clothes.

Zaf stood back, suppressing a laugh. "You want a photo?"

"We sure do," said Arwen.

Zaf took her phone, resisting the urge to tell the hens they looked more like Superman than Bridget. They crowded in for a group hug beneath the red awnings of the stationery shop, took dozens of selfies and then dispersed, giggling.

"Well I never," murmured Diana. "I hope they plan to take those off if they want to be taken seriously in the shops."

Zaf shrugged. He was sure the store owners had seen worse.

"Well, I've just spotted somewhere I can buy a new cravat," said Stuart. "I shall see you all in a moment."

"I'll stay out here," said Zaf to Diana, "so everyone knows where to meet."

Diana nodded and went into the Montblanc shop with the larger part of the group.

Zaf wandered over to an ornate covered drinking fountain and leaned against it.

"So, Mr Tour Guide," said Tom, strolling over with a grin, "know some exciting facts about this 'ere drinking fountain?"

Zaf puffed out his chest. "It was built to commemorate the jubilee of the Metropolitan Drinking Fountain and Cattle Trough Association."

"You just made that up."

"God's truth."

"Cattle Trough Association?"

"A very important body. I'm afraid the fountain doesn't work."

"Form without function. Doesn't matter how snazzy it looks. If the thing doesn't work, what's the point of it?"

Tom circled the fountain and shook his head. "This thing is bigger than some bedsits I've seen. It's insane that it's taking up all this space and serving no purpose."

"Tell me about it," said Zaf.

"Which part? The expense of living in London or the taking up space and serving no purpose?" asked Tom.

"Both," said Zaf. "Hey, maybe when your Bifrost thing is a worldwide success, they'll put up a memorial to you."

Tom laughed. "I think Cat is more likely to just pay me what I'm owed." He reached out and took Zaf's fingers lightly in his. "I enjoyed last night."

"Me too."

"I'm not sure if I've ever gone a date that's involved creeping up and down residential streets looking for lucky horseshoes and posting cryptic notes through doors. Very clandestine stuff."

"It's a secret mission for later," said Zaf. "A mission to locate the mysterious Pascal."

Tom held onto his fingers. "We're all still in London until tomorrow. We could... meet again tonight."

Zaf gestured towards the shop. "It's Diana's birthday. Special barbecue tonight."

"Oh, happy birthday to her." Tom sounded disappointed. He pointed at the shop window. "And they're *not* the mother and daughter?"

Zaf frowned, then realised what Tom was talking about. Through the glass, Lydia and Arwen were posing with a fancy diary. Arwen was handing the book to Lydia as if it was a gift.

"No," said Zaf. "That's just her friend, Lydia. London friend. Her London 'mum', if you like."

"Right," said Tom, getting out his phone. "Because – and I don't want you thinking I stalk people on social media, OK? – but if you look at Arwen Griffith's extensive social media posts, she's very much positioning Lydia there as her real mum."

"Really?"

Tom flipped to an open app. His social media tag was *@TomBuildsBridges*. He scrolled through reel after reel of photos of Arwen and Lydia.

"So, Arwen's telling the world that Lydia's her actual mum?" Zaf said.

"She's doing what?"

Zaf turned to see Gaynor sitting on a nearby stone block bench, sipping her nutritious smoothie.

"I'm..." Zaf began. "I'm sure it's not what it seems."

Chapter Forty

As Arwen and her gaggle of friends emerged from the shop with their purchases, the furious Gaynor pushed herself up with effort.

She marched on Arwen. "Why on earth would you do such a cruel thing? Is your own mother too... what? Shabby? Ugly? Ill?"

"What? Mum..."

Gaynor was holding Tom's phone. She thrust it at her daughter. "This. When did you start telling the world Lydia was your mum?"

Arwen stared back at Gaynor. "It's not like that, Mum. It's playing up to an image, that's all."

"An image I don't fit into."

"Stop it! You're making this into a much bigger deal than it needs to be!"

"Can I just say I've never felt comfortable with it?" put in Lydia.

"Shut up!" Gaynor snapped. "You're not part of this family!"

"I... I bought you a diary by the way," said Arwen, offering a gift bag to Gaynor.

"No you didn't! You bought a diary for your stunt mother. I don't want something that's been re-gifted."

"You're being crazy now! I bought it for you because you lost yours and I felt bad for you." Arwen waved the bag at her mum.

"Oh! Oh! Feel bad for me, do you? Am I something to be pitied, after all I've done for you?" Gaynor clutched her handbag. "I don't want that diary and I don't need it. I found my diary this morning, under the other bed in our room."

"You did?" said Bethan.

Arwen sagged. "Well, this is an extra diary."

"An extra diary for your extra mum, huh?"

"Please, Mum! You're making a scene!"

"Isn't that what you want?" Gaynor gestured at the women, all of them still wearing their Bridget Jones knickers over their clothes. "Isn't it always about causing a scene?! Why can't you be more like your sister?"

Bethan gasped.

Arwen jabbed a finger at her mum. "Be more like Bethan? You want two sad stay-at-home daughters with gambling problems who get no joy from life and have no lives of their own?"

Zaf caught movement from the corner of his eye: Diana emerging from the shop with the last of the group. From the look on her face, she'd heard it all.

"Well now! It's time to move on!" she said with forced cheeriness. "How about we take in London Bridge, Southwark Bridge and make our way to our wine bar stop?"

There was no response from the hen party. Ther group looked variously shocked, angered and embarrassed.

Stuart Dinktrout appeared at the edge of the group, looking delighted with himself. "So, who wants to see my new cravat?"

His smile dropped as he realised no one cared.

Zaf was grateful to get the fractious group back on the bus. Yes, it meant they were confined together in a small space, but it also meant he and Diana could hide behind the safety of the microphone and throw out distracting facts as they wended their away across two of the Thames' grand bridges and on to their final tour destination.

Newton drove them back across the river into Borough. Now that they'd put some physical and emotional distance between themselves and the diary shop argument, Zaf hoped the group might benefit from a little relaxation. For now, the hen party sat in brittle silence.

"We'll be arriving at the wine bar shortly," he announced as they crossed over to the south of the river once more. "It's on Bedale Street, where we saw Bridget's flat above the pub before. At the wine bar there are cocktails named after the principal characters in the film, so perhaps you need to work out whether you want a taste of Mark Darcy or Daniel Cleaver?"

No response. Things *were* bad.

Off the bus and into the bar they went. Zaf found himself counting the party off the bus, something that had proven singularly difficult the last time they were on this road.

The venue had high ceilings and gentle lighting. The enormous brick archways were part of a railway bridge, partly plastered over and painted with ancient-looking murals. There were nooks populated by lush green plants, and higher up, the walls contained racks of wine bottles.

Everyone seemed keen for a drink, and moments later the group settled into a loose cluster in the comfy seating.

Arwen lounged on a sofa flanked by her hens, all of them studying the cocktail menu. Gaynor sat at a distance, smarting from the earlier exchange.

Bethan's face was grim, but she was clearly attempting to put on a brave face. "The Daniel Cleaver sounds nice," she said with little enthusiasm. "Grand Marnier, orange juice and sparkling wine. A Mimosa, really."

"Why does it say there might be an unpleasant surprise lurking below that smooth exterior?" asked Lydia. "I don't see how a cocktail could two-time you."

Bethan shrugged. "Well, I'm having one."

"In case cocktails aren't your thing," Zaf said, "there's wine and craft beers too."

He glanced over at the bridge group to see Tom already at the bar, a tall glass of beer being placed in front of him. Stuart and Bunty were arguing about wine.

"I don't know why you insist on Burgundy," said Stuart. "It's overpriced, because of the name. You must see that!"

"Because of the name? Do you hear what you just said?" Bunty put a mocking hand to his ear. "Because of the name? Do you even know what an appellation is?"

"*Appellation d'Origine Contrôlée.*" Stuart puffed out his chest. "*Naturellement.*"

Bunty grimaced. "Or AOC as we might say if we weren't torturing a beautiful language for sport. Which is the French way of saying that the location is what matters. They are very terroir-conscious, it's true. If you want quality, you must pay for it."

Once he'd checked that everyone was happily settled, Zaf wandered over to join Tom at the bar.

"What can I get you?" Tom said. "I'm ready for a refill."

"I'm tempted to have a glass of whatever you're having," Zaf replied, "but I'm still responsible for the group. So I'll take a soda water for now, thanks."

"You're a cheap date! You know, when Bifrost takes off I'm gonna be properly flush. Sure you don't want something more than that?"

Zaf shook his head. "I hope it does take off, Tom. You have such a passion for it."

"As do these kind gents who have been kind enough to invest. They see the vision, or at least, they're confident that I can see it."

Tom raised his beer in the direction of Stuart and Bunty, now standing by a map of France's wine regions on the wall and arguing.

"They're so funny," said Zaf. "So much in common, and yet they're arguing."

"So much in common? Don't let them hear you say that. I think it's just their way of talking, to be honest. Both of them are used to being the loudest voice in the room."

"Well thank goodness they listened to you and your Bifrost proposal," said Zaf. He raised his soda water. "Cheers!"

Chapter Forty One

Diana stood at the end of the bar, glancing over to check that the group was settled.

Zaf and Tom were enjoying a chat which she didn't want to disturb. The hens were piling into the cocktails. Nearby, Stuart and Bunty were engaged in an animated discussion that seemed to relate to the map of France on the wall.

"Is this a wine conversation?" Diana asked.

"It most certainly is," said Stuart. "Let me explain. This map is a useful tool, it shows all of the wine producing areas of France."

She looked up at it. "All of them?"

A nod. "Now here in the east, we have Bunty's beloved Burgundy, see? It's a well-known and highly overrated wine-producing region. And on the west, we have Bordeaux. Wines that are just as good, but Bunty's not having any of that, because of his wine snobbery."

"Steady on old chap!" Bunty interjected.

"*People who know choose Bordeaux.* They used to say

that on adverts and I've never forgotten." Stuart tapped the side of his head.

"Oh, it was on an advert?" Bunty said with a snort. "It must be true then!"

"It's stood me in good stead through the years."

"Can I add something to the conversation?" Diana asked.

The two men looked confused.

"By all means," said Stuart. "I'm sure we can probably answer any questions between us."

Diana lifted her duck-head umbrella to use as a pointer.

"Both of these regions have a strong and ancient tradition of making fine wine." She tapped Burgundy. "Here in Burgundy they lean into the purity and individual character of a vineyard." She tapped on the left. "Over in Bordeaux, more blending occurs, perhaps at the chateau level, or more widely. Still confusing, though. That old advertising campaign will have been playing to the idea of higher volumes and perhaps some sense of consistency."

Bunty looked triumphant. "Populist, you mean."

"What of the grape varieties?" Diana continued. "Pinot noir dominates in Burgundy for red wines. In Bordeaux they use multiple grape varieties. Comparing them is perhaps a foolish endeavour." She looked up into the stunned faces of each man. "Or of course, it can be a topic of endless conversation, if that's what entertains you."

"We were just trying to agree on a bottle to drink between us," said Stuart, looking deflated. "Help us decide?"

Diana pulled out the menu and pointed to an entry. "I recommend this one."

Bunty gasped. "From Chile?"

She nodded. "Chile rescued one of France's most precious grape varieties, without anyone knowing for many years," said Diana. "The Carménère grape was rendered more or less extinct in France in the nineteenth century by a pest. Cuttings were exported, but misidentified for decades as Merlot."

"Good grief, imagine!" Bunty clasped his hands. "So the grape is saved, and they're replanting it in France?"

Diana shrugged. "It seems they know exactly what to do with it in Chile. You should try it."

Chapter Forty-Two

Zaf had thought that Tom was uninhibited enough when sober, but he was rapidly becoming tipsy as he downed another pint.

"Your colleague Diana's just rocked their world, going by their body language," Tom said, nodding over at Stuart and Bunty.

"She does that. People underestimate her."

Tom nodded.

"Mind you," Zaf continued, "I may have a surprise lined up for her birthday. One she'll never see coming. It's not often I get to surprise her."

"Is this to do with all that sneaking around in Holland Park last night?"

"It is. I happened to glance at one of Diana's old diaries and saw references to an old boyfriend, Pascal. She's never talked about him but I popped that note through his door and, yeah, if he texts me, then he's coming to the party. A wonderful reunion. I can't wait!" Zaf smiled at the thought.

Tom cocked his head. "You really care about people,

don't you? Not just Diana, I mean all of us. You work so hard to make people happy."

"I like doing those things. I like people."

Tom made a deep noise of contentment. "It's nice that this should end on a high note."

"End?"

Tom leaned in and kissed him lightly. After what seemed like an age, he pulled away, his eyes roaming Zaf's face.

"It doesn't need to end, I suppose," he said. "I mean, I've got to go to Spain after this. There's various complicated manufacturing things to set up. But that's only for a while. *This...*" He took hold of Zaf's hands. "Afterwards, I would very much like to pick up this little adventure where we left off."

Before Zaf could respond, Bethan let out a shriek.

"A gherkin! In the bottom of the glass! It scared me half to death!"

"That's your Daniel Cleaver, right there!" said one of the women. "A nasty surprise lurking below the smooth exterior."

Even Gaynor, still smarting from the stationery shop exchange, cracked a smile. Arwen saw and waved her over.

"Come on, Mum. Order a cocktail."

Gaynor shuffled from her chair and joined the rest of the hen party.

Zaf realised Tom was speaking again.

"I meant it was nice this tour ends on a high note after the sad death of whatsisface. David."

"A man we barely knew," Zaf said. A thought crossed his mind. "Ever heard of the Pale Horse?"

"Pardon?" said Tom.

"The Pale Horse. It was on a note. Thought it might be a pub."

"It's a Bible quote," said Tom.

"That's what I said."

"And an Agatha Christie book, too."

Zaf blinked. "It is?"

"Sure it is." Tom frowned. "Not sure how I know. Someone must have mentioned it." He patted Zaf on the arm. "Right, best mingle. And then I've got an announcement to make."

He moved off through the crowd.

Zaf took out his phone and googled *Pale Horse*.

"*... a mysterious thriller in which a group of people investigates a series of seemingly unrelated deaths, leading them to a clandestine organization and a deadly conspiracy...*"

He would tell Diana later. Maybe it meant nothing. Maybe David Medawar had just been making a note of a future book he wanted to read.

The hen group were laughing loudly, and there was a flurry of selfies being taken. Intrigued, Zaf flipped apps and tried to find Arwen Griffiths' social media feeds. Arwen and Lydia had indeed set themselves up as a social media mother and daughter, two glamorous and slender women constantly enjoying the best that the capital had to offer. Arwen had even added some of the photos that the misdirected wedding photographer had taken at the Redhouse Hotel.

As he scrolled through the photos, there was the loud tapping of a glass. He looked up to see that Tom had climbed onto a chair to address everyone.

"Get down!" called the woman behind the bar.

"In a moment, please," Tom said. "Everyone, I just wanted to say a few words. Words of gratitude." He spread his arms wide. "In many ways this has been an awful weekend, a bloody awful weekend, but I think you'll all agree that our fine tour guides, Zaf and Diana, have pulled out all the stops to make it as un-awful as possible."

There was spontaneous applause. Zaf felt his cheeks heat up in surprise.

"*And*," said Tom, "a handsome little bird has told me that it's someone's special day today. Diana turns... how many years old is it, Diana?"

"None of your business!"

There was laughter.

"Let's all wish Diana the very happiest of birthdays from her grateful tour party!" Tom said. "And now you need to get off and enjoy your barbecue."

"Barbecue sounds lovely," said Bunty.

"We should gatecrash it!" declared one of the hens.

"I don't think so..." Diana said.

"I'll bring the wine," said Stuart. "A vanload."

"That's really very generous." Diana was looking wary. Zaf wondered if he should step in.

"Oh, it's decided then?" said Arwen.

"Where's it happening?" asked Tom.

"Er." Diana looked uneasy. "Eccleston Square. Pimlico."

"That's dead classy, that is," said Arwen.

Tom raised his glass. "This party is never going to stop!" He spotted the look on the barmaid's face and jumped down to the floor.

Zaf mouthed a *sorry* to Diana. She raised an eyebrow in return and moved through the crowd towards him.

"Oh, God, I'm so, so sorry," he said. "I didn't mean to do this."

A shrug. "You told a man it was my birthday. That's not a crime."

"Still..."

"Still," she agreed. "I like people. You know I like people. But the guest list for this party has just gone from eighty to a hundred."

A hundred and one, thought Zaf, thinking of Pascal.

"We might need to reconsider the catering situation." She looked at her watch. "We should get this lot back to the hotel soon. We'll be setting up in the garden in the next couple of hours. Meanwhile, I need to let Levon know we'll need more food. Which you're paying for, of course."

Zaf swallowed. "Of course."

She smiled: she didn't mean it. *Thank goodness.*

Diana turned to the tour party. "Last orders, everyone. Then it's back to the bus if you want a ride back to the hotel."

Chapter Forty-Three

The guests had managed to tuck away a surprising number of drinks in the wine bar. As they left, Gaynor was making threatening gestures to a man who was trying to get Bethan's attention. Diana took her by the arm and steered her onto the bus.

They crossed over Tower Bridge one last time in the direction of the hotel.

"Am I to hang around and drive them over to your barbecue in Eccleston Square later?" Newton asked.

Diana surveyed the group.

"No. I think a walk, even just to the tube station, will do them good. And perhaps put some of them off."

"Right you are."

Gaynor was now fanning herself with one hand and chugging down the remainder of her daily smoothie with the other.

"Go easy, Mum," said Arwen.

"I need to get my strength back up."

"It's a nutrient drink, not a magic anti-drunkenness potion," said Lydia.

Gaynor glared at her. "How old are you supposed to be, anyway?"

"I'm fifty."

"So as her 'fake mum', you had her before you were even twenty."

Lydia shrugged.

Gaynor eyed her. "You don't look a day over forty, though."

"Um. Thank you."

"It's down to a good skin care regime, I guess."

"Perhaps. Or maybe I've not done anything with my life," said Lydia with a sad note to her voice.

Gaynor grunted and pointed at herself. "It's not the years but the miles that do the damage. It's been a whirlwind. And soon there'll be nothing left of me and just a big old empty house to leave to my girls."

"Mum!" said Arwen.

"Oh, don't worry. We'll get to your wedding. I'll manage that much."

Diana watched Gaynor's face, noting how small and tired she seemed.

The bus pulled up outside the Redhouse Hotel and the guests piled off.

"We will be at your residence within the hour," Stuart said to Diana. "With the finest wines money can buy."

"Chosen by me," added Bunty.

"Two hours will be soon enough," Diana said.

The group disappeared inside and Newton drove the bus the short distance to the Chartwell and Crouch depot.

The depot manager, Paul Kensington, was hovering

outside his own office. Diana didn't have much time for the man, but was intrigued by his presence.

"Everything alright, Paul?"

"There were police here the other day."

Did he look scared?

"Yes, I know."

"They were in my office, Miss Bakewell. I saw them. Forensic people in their suits with their yellow tape."

"No," she said, "I think you're wrong. They were just doing the bus. The police are still investigating the murder of David Medawar."

"That's what they told me. I came back later and all the stuff was gone. Newton Crombie and Mr Williams told me they'd never been in here."

"Exactly. You must have been confused."

"Confused? Not me. But look."

He moved closer the door and pointed.

In the centre of the room, next to Paul's ridiculous tiny Japanese Zen garden, was Gus the tabby cat.

"That's Gus," Diana said.

"I know that," Paul muttered. "But what's he looking at?"

Gus seemed to be staring at a point in space above Paul's desk.

"He's probably looking at a fly or a spider," Diana suggested.

"Can you see a fly or a spider? I can't. They say cats can see things that are beyond human reckoning."

Human reckoning?

She frowned. "Are you suggesting Gus is looking at a ghost?"

Paul gasped. "Can you see it?"

Diana pushed down a sigh. "Can I see the ghost that's

not there and which Gus is almost certainly not looking at, because he's probably just looking at an ant or something? No, Paul. I cannot."

"You're a sceptic. I see that. But sometimes there are things that not everyone can see. There are more things on—"

"Possibly," Diana interrupted, "but I don't think there's a ghost here. If you'll excuse me, I have some catering to sort out."

Paul Kensington waved her away.

Diana wandered over to Zaf, scrolling through her phone for a number as she did.

"I've got some social media photos I have to show you," he said.

"I thought you were trying to be less shallow."

He tensed. "They're not mine."

"No? Very well. Anyway, you know those CSI London games you were playing in Paul's office the other day?"

"Yeah," said Zaf.

"It seems to have ended up with Paul believing there's been a murder in there, and Gus can see the victim's ghost."

Zaf laughed. "He's *what?*"

Diana held up a hand. She'd found the number she was after. Levon, from the *Tasty for You* café, picked up.

"Levon. Um, a little change of plan. We've got some extra guests coming for the barbecue."

Levon sounded out of breath. "How many?" he panted.

"Twenty."

"Twenty?"

"Twenty. And I was wondering about the sausage situation. Do we have enough food to go round?"

"For another twenty?"

"Another twenty."

"You know it is not just sausages, don't you?"

"I do."

He made a teeth-sucking noise. "I doubt there's enough for that many people."

"Then I need to get some more food," Diana said.

"I'll be starting to cook soon. It's not all just sausages, you know."

"I know."

Diana hung up. Why had she told the tour group where the party was?

Chapter Forty-Four

Diana looked at Zaf. "We need more food to accommodate your extra guests."

"*My* extra guests?" He opened his mouth to object, then shook his head. "Let's pop to the supermarket."

"I've a better idea." She scrolled through her contacts again and called Big Ernie Holland.

Big Ernie picked up halfway through a laugh. "Alright, Diana darling. Just been talking about you."

"Have you now?"

Diana smiled. Ernie was a constant, solid presence in her life. She knew he was, to use Zaf's description, 'a bit dodgy', and probably more than that. But he was a man she could turn to at any time.

"I'll be over at your gaff in a bit," he said. "Everything alright?"

"I've got a minor food emergency."

She explained the details.

"You come over here," Ernie told her, "and I'll have a fine

selection of products for you. I know a man who owes me a favour or two."

"That's great. But I don't know if I've got time to come to you."

"It's alright. My lad, Chaz, is in the area. He's coming to pick you up."

"Don't put yourself out."

"He's just around the corner. See you in minute, sweetheart."

Ernie ended the call.

"You've gone to Big Ernie for the barbecue?" Zaf said.

"He knows people."

"I'm not sure I like some of the people he knows. Is he sending an ominous black cab to pick us up?"

Diana smiled. "How did you know?"

She went outside to find a black London hackney cab already waiting, a shaven-headed thug behind the wheel. Chaz Chase, Ernie's gofer and general dogsbody.

"Afternoon, Chaz," she said as she climbed into the back.

He looked at her in the mirror. "Hear you've got a catering emergency."

Zaf was climbing in after her. Diana frowned at him.

"An extra pair of hands," he said.

Diana nodded and looked back at Chaz. "And not much time."

"Then get your boy strapped in and hold onto your valuables. I'll be putting me foot down."

Despite the warning, Chaz never once exceeded the speed limit. However, his interpretation of red traffic lights and who had right of way at junctions became more and more flexible as the journey went on.

Zaf pressed himself into his seat and held his phone out to her.

"Ah, your social media pictures," she said.

"Not mine," he reminded her. "This is Arwen's feed."

She took the phone and flicked through the images. The past two-and a-bit days had yielded hundreds of images, each of them with hundreds of likes.

"She's certainly popular," Diana said.

"Go back," Zaf told her. "Go right back."

"Am I looking for something specific?"

She went back to the first morning of the tour. Arwen had uploaded photos that made it look like an intimate, almost private, event for just her and Lydia. The images had joy but no soul. They were beautiful, bland and forgettable.

"I'd be annoyed too," she said, "if my daughter airbrushed me out of her life."

Zaf leaned over. "Where are you up to?"

Diana had gone back to the very first morning and a group picture of the women. They were all putting on their best duck-face pouts for the camera. Gaynor was right on the edge of the shot, with Bethan in her arm cast and sling beside her.

"You've gone too far," Zaf said. "Scoot forward. "It's one that wedding photographer did. There."

She stopped. The image was one of several of the hen party posing in the function room.

"Yes?" she said.

"Look at the table," Zaf told her.

There was a carrier bag on the table, the one Gaynor had been given to replace the handbag the police had taken for testing.

"Then go back one," he said.

Diana flicked back one shot, then forward to the original one. She repeated this a few times.

She could see what Zaf was referring to.

Gaynor's purple diary was poking out of the bag on the first image, but missing from the second.

Zaf pointed at the image. "That's when her diary disappeared. She said she found it under the bed in her room. But someone took it from her bag between the times those two photos were taken."

"But what does that mean?" Diana said.

"I don't know. But that's when it happened."

"Right in front of everyone. When we were all together."

Zaf looked out at London whizzing by as they drove into the East End.

"Cat at Tower not in diary," he mused.

Diana shook her head. "It doesn't make sense."

As they passed through St Anne's Church in Limehouse, there was a glimpse of the pyramid-topped tower of Canary Wharf visible through the trees. Zaf gasped.

"Cat at Tower not in diary!" he said. "Cat. Cat... oh, what's her name? Catherine. Cat. Tom's called her that himself."

"Tower Division Engineering," Diana said. "Catherine Garratt at Tower Division Engineering. Not in diary. That's it!"

Chapter Forty-Five

Zaf frowned. "Why would David have expected Catherine whatserface to be in Gaynor's diary?"

"Was he writing about her diary?" Diana asked. "And how does that link to the Pale Horse?"

"Tom pointed that one out to me. It's an Agatha Christie book."

"Of course." *That* was why it had seemed familiar. "So, check an Agatha Christie novel because Catherine Garratt at Tower Division Engineering is not in the diary?"

"It doesn't make sense," Zaf said. "And what would David Medawar know about Gaynor's diary, anyway? He'd never seen it."

Diana remembered something.

"Actually, he might have done."

"Really?"

"Bethan said David had shown an interest in Gaynor's illness when they spoke the night before he died."

"Yes?"

"And Stuart – yes, I think it was Stuart – said he saw

David walking to the lifts with a hardback book in his hand later that evening."

Zaf pulled himself up higher in the cab seat. "Gaynor's diary?"

She nodded. "Could be."

"So he was the one who stole it."

Diana shook her head. "She had it the next morning, after David had died." She gestured at Zaf's phone. "Those pictures show it was stolen while everyone was in the room."

"But he did have it the night before he died..." Zaf frowned. "If he had it, then..."

"What if Gaynor had given it to him? To read?"

"Why would she do that?"

Diana gazed out of the window of the cab. They were past the City now, heading east. "Gaynor Griffiths has never been shy about her illness and her experiences. She'd probably relish giving it to him to read."

"But why would a... what was he? A Brazilian-born chemical engineer want with a Welsh woman's cancer diary?"

Diana had no answer to that. Besides, they had arrived.

The cab pulled up outside Auntie Lipman's, a greasy spoon café on a dingy road in the East End. Emerging from the shop, bearing a massive metal platter, was Big Ernie. The smallest 'big' man Diana had ever known, at least since his recent health kick.

Diana stepped out of the cab to greet him. She struggled to hug him around the huge tray.

"Diana love, prepare yourself for a feast fit for kings. Homemade beef burgers, succulent Caribbean chicken burgers, maple barbecue sausages, some little pork bad boys, and if you're feeling adventurous, five of these pork, chilli and garlic ones."

She smiled. "Quite the selection."

Ernie laughed. "We're just getting started, love. How about some French garden herb chicken kebabs, some lamb koftas that'll transport you to the Mediterranean and some pork and pineapple kebabs that are a tropical de-light?"

"You've outdone yourself, Ernie."

Ernie winked. "Oi, oi, Zaf, me lad. And here, as a Brucie bonus, a full rack of baby back ribs that'll 'ave you licking your fingers."

"Where did you get this from?" Zaf asked.

Ernie gave him an indecipherable look. "A bloke owes me a favour."

Zaf grimaced, no doubt expecting to find a severed finger or two in there.

"This is a wonder, Ernie," Diana said.

"Well, it's not every day my niece has a birthday."

"Not your real niece," said a woman coming out of the shop.

It took Diana a moment to recognise her. It had been quite a few years, and the woman had dyed her hair a vibrant colour.

"Ariadne."

"Happy birthday, darling." Ariadne took hold of Diana's shoulders to give her a kiss on the cheek.

Diana stiffened.

"You girls play nice," muttered Ernie. He gave Zaf an apologetic look. "This is my niece – my real niece, I guess. Ariadne. Ariadne, Zaf."

Ariadne gave him a warm smile. The years had been kind to her, Diana noted.

"You work for Chartwell and Crouch, I think?" said Ariadne, looking at Zaf's uniform. "It's good to meet you."

"She's with the competition," Ernie said.

"Competition?" asked Zaf.

Ariadne laughed. "He means ACE tours."

"I've heard of them," Zaf said, nodding. Diana prayed he wouldn't mention that they'd stolen the idea for the Bridget Jones tours off ACE Tours.

"If you ever want to move up in the world..." Ariadne gave Zaf a wink. She tossed Diana a smile and went back into the shop.

"Put the meat in the car," Diana told Zaf, aware of the tension in her voice.

"I'll be along in a bit," said Ernie.

"Just you?" Diana looked past him at the café.

"Yeah. Just me," he said, then grinned. "Maybe Chaz."

"Chaz, of course."

"Your old mum coming?" Ernie asked.

"You know she doesn't like to leave the East End."

"It's only Pimlico."

"That's *here be dragons* as far as my mum is concerned," said Diana.

She and Zaf got back in the cab with the food perched on the seat between them. Chaz set off and they drove in silence, Diana gathering her thoughts.

"Ariadne back there," she began. "Ariadne and me..."

"You don't have to say anything."

She glanced at Zaf. Sometimes, he could be very mature.

"She's from my past," she explained. "We were best friends. School and after. And then things..."

"People have pasts. Complicated ones. I should think if we tot up all the positive relationships you've created and take away all the broken ones, you'll still have a very healthy balance in the friendship bank."

She reached over and squeezed his arm. "You're too nice, Zaf. You know that?"

"Uh-huh," he said. "I'd like you to remember that the next time I finish the mayo and don't buy a replacement."

She smiled. "Maybe."

Chapter Forty-Six

As the black cab dropped Zaf and Diana back at Eccleston Square, Zaf noticed activity in the huge garden at its centre.

Friends and neighbours were putting up a marquee complete with chairs, tables and a sound system. Nichola, a local resident who seemed to tend the garden full time, had a set of step ladders and was stringing bunting and fairy lights between the trees. Zaf was starting to get an idea of how big this party might be.

"We might want to get changed," Diana said. "The party appears to be starting imminently. But first..." She pointed across the gardens with her duck-headed umbrella. "Levon is setting up over there."

Zaf went over with the heaped trays of barbecue supplies.

Levon, owner and manager of the *Tasty for You* café, had brought what looked like half his kitchen. Crockery and cutlery for more than a hundred people was stacked besides covered trays of bread rolls, salads and accompaniments. Two large oil-barrel barbecues were smoking gently.

His eyes lit up as he spotted Zaf with the trays. "Thanks." He grabbed the trays and started working through their contents.

"There's a lot of sausages," he said.

"People like sausages," Zaf replied.

He hurried across the road to the house to get dressed, nearly colliding with Alexsei coming out. Alexsei wore a tailored jacket and a crisp white shirt so bright it made his wavy black hair seem even more lustrous.

"Looking sharp," Zaf said.

"I try." Alexsei looked Zaf up and down in his work gear.

"I'm getting changed!" Zaf said.

A shrug. "I like you just the way you are."

Zaf ran upstairs, wondering if he'd heard right.

Diana was in the hallway of their flat, crouched by a bookcase.

"Er, party?" he said.

"Just reading." She held up a book. It was a tatty and elderly paperback, almost falling apart at the bindings. The cover had an image of a pub sign featuring a rearing white horse.

"*The Pale Horse*," she said. "I knew I had it somewhere."

"Still," Zaf said. "There's a party..."

She waved him away. "Get ready. Go down there. Help put cushions on the chairs please. There should be some blankets that we can hang on the backs for when it gets cooler later."

"Make sure all the guests are comfy, got it."

Zaf washed and changed as swiftly as he could and then,

slipping past Diana, who was still inspecting the Agatha Christie novel, hurried down to the garden.

The sun was shining and the garden looked amazing. Barbecue smells wafted across the space.

Zaf helped a woman arrange cushions on the marquee seats and it wasn't until she said his name that Zaf recognised her.

"Carolyn. You took us mudlarking the other month."

"Didn't recognise me without my wellies and practical trousers on?" she replied.

She wore a brightly coloured sundress, in contrast to the very practical gear she'd worn on the foreshore of the Thames when picking through the mud for hidden treasures.

"I can't believe you can tear yourself away from the river," he said. "It must be addictive."

"Tide's in." She winked and went back to putting out cushions.

Zaf looked around at the gardens, wondering what else needed doing. As he was about to approach Nichola and her bunting, a van pulled up.

The logo told him the van belonged to a wine wholesaler.

He smiled. *Thank you, Stuart Dinktrout.*

Crates of wine were unloaded, and within ten minutes, there was a table loaded with champagne glasses, ready to welcome the guests.

Zaf watched the van leave, thinking of Tom. He'd be here soon, as a guest.

He sent off a text. *Looking forward to seeing you shortly. Can't stop thinking about you!*

It was a while since he'd felt himself falling for someone like this. Before Malachi, there had been Nicholas in Birmingham, but that had gone pear-shaped when Nicholas had gone to Stirling for uni while Zaf had come here.

It was good to feel like this again.

He flipped to Tom's social media – *TomBuildsBridges* – and flicked through, admiring the exploits of that most charming and handsome man.

Chapter Forty-Seven

Diana closed the copy of *The Pale Horse* and stood up.

She considered it while she freshened up and got changed. She thought long and hard, then came to a decision.

She picked up her phone and called DCI Clint Sugarbrook.

It might have been a Sunday, but he picked up before the third ring. "DCI Sugarbrook."

"Detective Sugarbrook, it's Diana Bakewell. I hope I'm not interrupting anything."

There was a squeal in the background and the shout of children's voices.

"Sunday is normally a day of rest," he replied in an even tone. "How can I help you?"

"It's about David Medawar. I think I know who murdered him."

A pause. "You have information you'd like to share? You know who killed him?"

Diana pulled a face. "I don't *know* who killed him, but I have an idea why he was killed."

"Ah, a theory." Sugarbrook sighed.

Diana wasn't about to let him put her off. "David Medawar had a strong analytical mind. He was clearly a clever man. He had come to London to confront someone. That's by the by. Detective, are you familiar with thallium poisoning?"

"Thallium?" Sugarbrook huffed. "David Medawar was strangled, Miss Bakewell. Very clearly. There's even white cotton fibres on his neck from the cord that was used."

"That somewhat confirms it."

"Confirms it? Our murder victim was strangled, not poisoned."

"Ah yes, but that's because we were probably looking at the wrong murder all along. It makes a lot more sense if you look at it from the other direction."

She could almost hear his frown. "There were *two* murders?"

"I think so. And that's why David Medawar had to die."

"You aren't making a great deal of sense, Miss Bakewell. My family are here, I really—"

"Listen," she said. "I'm having a bit of a barbecue party in the gardens outside my house. Eccleston Square. If you – and your family – want to come over, I'd be delighted to see you. And the murderer should be along at any moment too."

Silence.

"Detective?"

A sigh. "Is there a vegetarian option?"

"Pardon?"

"My eldest is going through a vegetarian phase. Is there a vegetarian option at your barbecue?"

"Er... yes."

"Then we might come along. Or we might not."

That was the best she could hope for. Diana hung up and checked herself in the mirror before going out to join her birthday party.

The sun was shining and friends from across London were here celebrating with her. She saw the city as an extended village of friends and colleagues, and every once in a while she got the chance to see them all together. Tea dresses and linen shirts fluttered in the faint breeze and people sipped at the chilled drinks with appreciation.

She made sure to speak to everyone as they arrived. Some brought her a gift, even though she had urged them not to. Her favourites were home-made jams and pickles; no waste there.

The men of the bridge tour party arrived with Stuart and Bunty at their head.

"So very good to see you," Diana said. "I see we've had a delivery from the wine bar. A whole crate of the Carménère."

"Marvellous," said Bunty. "Point us right at it, eh?"

The men moved on and a swell of noise announced the arrival of the Bridget Jones hen party.

"Bethan, Natalie, Phoebe." Diana greeted them all in turn and directed them to the drinks and food. She gave Gaynor a hug and indicated the smoothie drink sticking out of the woman's handbag. "You can forget that for tonight. Drinks are over there."

Arwen and Lydia were hanging back outside the garden gate, caught up in their own conversation.

"It's just not working anymore," Lydia said.

"It's working just fine," Arwen replied. "The number of

shared likes we're getting. People love the mum and daughter thing."

"I'm sorry. It's like your mum said."

"Ignore what my mum said. She'll get over it."

"I think she's been quite reasonable about the whole thing. But if I look forty, like your mum says, then the whole mum and daughter narrative doesn't work."

"Of course it works. And when people say we look like sisters that's just a thing people say to glamorous mums and daughters."

Lydia shook her head. "How long will it be before people look at this mum and daughter act and can't work out which one is meant to be the mum and which the daughter?"

"Hey! There's no way I look older than you," said Arwen.

"Look in a mirror, babycakes. Time is catching up on you."

Through the garden railings, Diana saw Arwen's mouth widen in shock. "You cow."

Lydia tilted her head. "It was fun while it lasted." She turned on her heel and walked away into the night.

Chapter Forty-Eight

Zaf spotted Newton standing at a table, picking hors d'oeuvres apart and dropping pieces onto the floor.

He looked down to see the grey tabby cat picking over the scraps. "You brought Gus?"

Newton nodded. "Seems as if he's a fan of smoked salmon."

Zaf resisted rolling his eyes at the man's devotion to his cat. He crouched and stroked the demanding moggy.

"Ah, now," said Newton. "There's the men I wanted to see." He marched towards a small cluster of the bridge group. "I've got some questions about this bridge project of yours."

"Too late to be an investor, dear fellow," Bunty said. "Deal's all sewn up."

"No. I meant about how it works, or rather, doesn't."

"Ah, well, then Tom's your man," said another. He waved a hand airily. "He's around here somewhere."

"Because I don't see how it could possibly function the way it's supposed to."

Zaf shrank back, wondering if Newton realised how rude he was being.

"Just watch the videos online," said Stuart. "Tom's prototypes show exactly how it works."

Zaf opened Tom's Instagram account and pulled up one of the videos. In it, Tom crouched low beneath a tropical sun discussing test number eighty-six. His prototype Bifrost system, no more than waist-high, fired bolts and cables across a muddy stream, then fed stronger cables and supports along the wire.

"The system won't work if the terrain is too soft or too hard," Newton said.

Stuart nodded sagely, a glass of white wine in his hand. "That was a tricky one for Tom to iron out, but the people at Tower Division were happy enough with the adjustments to buy the thing wholesale."

Zaf flicked back further. Video after video, amongst other snapshots of Tom's life. Watersports, fine restaurants...

He came to a picture that made him stop dead.

Zaf stepped backwards, almost colliding with Big Ernie, who was carrying a plate piled high with barbecue items.

"Oh. Hi Ernie."

"Nice spread, this." Ernie looked down at his full plate. "You alright, lad? You look like you've seen a ghost."

Zaf shook his head to dispel the shocking picture from his mind. "Sorry. Just been surprised by something."

Ernie nodded, then looked over Zaf's shoulder. "Oi-oi. Speaking of ghosts, here's a face I've not seen for a while."

Zaf turned to look.

A handsome older man wearing a fedora and linen suit had just walked through the gate. He tipped his hat towards Ernie, but didn't approach.

"Who's that?" asked Zaf.

"Pascal Palmer."

Zaf clenched a fist. *He came.* "That's Pascal?"

"A blast from the past. Used to be with my niece, Ariadne."

"But he knew Diana well."

"Oh, that he did. But it's complicated, best keep away."

"Sure," said Zaf, but walked over to Pascal nonetheless.

"Hello," he said. "You're Pascal Palmer."

The man seemed surprised. "I am."

Zaf put out a hand, then withdrew it, feeling ridiculous. "I'm Zaf. I work with Diana."

Pascal began to nod and then frowned. "Not at Chartwell and Crouch, surely?"

"Yes."

Pascal laughed. "She's not still there even after Morris Walker drove the place into the ground?"

"I... I wouldn't know. That was before my time."

"The man robbed the coffers with some fake ticket scheme. Fleeced thousands of customers. I thought the place had gone bankrupt."

Zaf had never met the former manager, Morris Walker. He'd only ever known Paul Kensington, but he'd heard enough chatter to be aware that Chartwell and Crouch were struggling and that somehow this Morris Walker character was responsible.

"You've not spoken to Diana in a while?" he asked.

"Must be more than a decade," Pascal replied.

"Oh? You were..." He hesitated. "You were close."

"Very much so. I don't know how I'd have got through that period of my life without her."

"I think she thought very highly of you."

Pascal tilted his head. "I wasn't necessarily under that same impression. Ah, and here she is."

Diana approached along the neatly edged footpath. As she recognised Pascal, she hesitated.

"Pascal?"

He removed his hat in greeting. "Diana. It's astonishing to see you."

"It's been a while."

"I'll admit, I was surprised to receive an invitation." He tapped his jacket pocket.

"Invitation." She frowned then looked at Zaf. "Holland Park. Zaf, is this anything to do with you?"

Zaf had the feeling he'd done something wrong. "Oh! Me? No." He cleared his throat. "I mean, yes."

"Oh," Pascal said. "I have been brought here under false pretences."

Diana was staring at Zaf. "What exactly was it that you were trying to do?"

Zaf fumbled for the words. "I wanted to do something special, y'know? Everything here was so carefully planned, but I thought I could maybe add a wow factor with an old flame."

"Old flame?" said Pascal.

"Old flame?" echoed Diana.

Zaf flicked a finger between them. "Old flames. You used to..."

There was a long pause, then Diana and Pascal burst out laughing.

"Oh Zaf, that's hilarious," said Diana, wiping a tear from her eye.

"Us?" Pascal's chest rocked with laughter. "Can you imagine?"

Zaf stared from one to the other, bewildered at how he could have got it so wrong.

Chapter Forty-Nine

Diana looked at Pascal, the coldness and surprise gone from her face. "Oh, Pascal. It really is a pleasure to see you."

Zaf watched her step forward, go up on tiptoes and put a kiss on his cheek.

"Whatever may have happened in the past, it's a delight to see you again," she said.

"And you," he replied.

With one hand still on Pascal's arm, Diana looked quizzically at Zaf.

"I can't imagine where you pulled this idea from, but no. Pascal and I have never been lovers."

"No?"

"Absolutely not."

"But... but..." Should he confess?

She looked at him, waiting for an explanation.

"When I put that stool from Bryan's flat in your room," Zaf said, "I accidentally knocked a shelf and a diary fell off... and I couldn't help but see."

Pascal smiled. "Secret diary entries about me?"

"The restaurants. The Enchanted Garden or whatever it was called. All those meals. You wrote that he needed you, Diana."

"You did?" said Pascal.

"You *did*," Diana said. "At the time."

"Picnics in the park. Him watching you. You two sneaking around so that..." Zaf realised he might have already said too much.

"Well, there was a bit of sneaking around," agreed Pascal. "I was married at the time and my wife would not have been very understanding. Have you seen Ariadne of late?" Pascal asked Diana.

"Never on purpose."

"So you *were* up to something," said Zaf. "You said something about worrying that your... antics might get into the newspaper."

"Well, I would hope they did," Pascal said.

"Huh?"

Diana patted the man's chest. "Zaf, Pascal's a restaurant critic, a food writer. The meals we shared were for his job."

"But he *needed* you."

Pascal smiled at Zaf. "I've been a recovering alcoholic for many years. Reviews of restaurants that serve alcohol, particularly with a pairing menu, require some commentary on the drinks. Diana's input was invaluable and I remain grateful to her."

Zaf tried to recall the words in the diary. The peculiar emphasis on the drinks. Pascal watching her face, the two of them trying to put their experiences into words.

"Oh," he said. "Oh."

"We were friends at the time, but things were difficult," said Diana. "Friendships fall apart."

"Marriages fail," said Pascal. "An unavoidable amount of sneaking around."

"Things shift and change and people drift apart."

"And it is clear," said Pascal, putting his hat back on, "that I was not meant to be at this party. Happy birthday, Diana. I bid you adieu."

"Not at all," she said firmly, holding onto his arm. "It was all a long, long time ago. Us. Morris. Ariadne. It's water under the bridge now."

He gave it some thought. "You're right. There's nothing to hide any more, is there?"

"We can start afresh. Now, go get yourself some food and then we can properly catch up."

She propelled Pascal away and looked at Zaf. "I should be so mad with you right now."

"I'm sorry. I just can't get anything right."

Diana pointed across the way. Tom Hatcher was crossing the garden, two bottles of beer in his hand, a smile on his face for Zaf.

"You get some things right," she said.

"Not even that," said Zaf miserably. "Excuse me."

He left her and went towards Tom. Tom's shirt was open to his chest and his sleeves rolled up. He looked like a millionaire on the deck of his Mediterranean yacht. He reached Zaf and leaned forward to kiss him but Zaf leaned back.

"Everything OK?" asked Tom.

"I saw something," Zaf said.

Tom frowned. "Something upset you?"

"I'm sure you can explain."

"I'll try."

Zaf got out his phone and went to Tom's social media feed. "This."

"The Bifrost test?"

Zaf swiped back an image. It showed Tom and a slender woman, both dressed in white beneath a shower of confetti, against the backdrop of a beautiful but crumbling white building that Zaf guessed was in Spain.

"Ah," said Tom.

"Ah?"

"Yes. That's Amelia."

"Go on," said Zaf.

"She's my... sister?"

Zaf swiped to an image of the happy couple sharing a kiss outside the church door.

"Ah," said Tom. "Um."

"You're married," said Zaf.

"Yes."

"I'm going to need a bit more than a simple *yes*," Zaf said.

"I... didn't say I *wasn't* married."

"You kissed me. We..." Zaf shook his head. "You said this thing wasn't going to end between us."

"And I meant that!" Tom said. "When I'm done with my business in Spain, I'll be back again and we can pick things up."

"Does business in Spain include Amelia?"

A shrug. "She *is* my wife."

"This wedding was recent."

"Six months ago."

"And you're already...?" Zaf grunted in disgust.

"We can make this work." Tom reached for Zaf's hand.

Zaf recoiled. "Does Amelia know?"

Tom laughed. "God, no. Can you imagine? My dirty little secret?" He reached out to touch Zaf.

Zaf stepped back. "This is over."

"It's barely begun."

"And I'm going to tell everyone why you murdered David Medawar," added Zaf, backing away.

"You... you what?" Tom spluttered.

Zaf gave him a glare and retreated through the dense garden.

He turned and ran to the little stage at the front of the marquee as if Tom Fletcher were hot on his heels. He stepped up, commandeered the microphone and turned to the crowd.

"Can I have everyone's attention, please," he said. "I've got something important to say."

Chapter Fifty

Diana had been checking on her guests when Zaf's voice came over the speaker system.

She stepped closer to the marquee and saw him on the little stage. He was gesturing to the man nearby to turn down the music.

"I've got something important to say," he repeated, sounding less certain now.

"Speech!" someone shouted.

Zaf stared blankly at the audience.

You can do this, Diana thought. He spent all day talking to large groups of strangers.

"I... I can't do this," he said, looking sickened.

"Sing us a song!" someone else shouted.

Diana watched Zaf's body language shift. He pulled on a big smile.

"I won't take up too much of your time. I'm Zaf. For those of you who don't know me, Diana has been kind enough to let me lodge with her over there." He pointed towards the flat. "I wanted to take this moment to wish Diana a very happy birthday."

There was a sprinkling of applause, and raised glasses.

"I'm not very good at this public speaking thing," Zaf continued. "I'm a fool. Other people tell me I'm better than that. They tell me I'm thoughtless and naïve, and that I'm terrible at sneaking into the house late. But, for some mad reason, they apparently like me the way I am. And I like them too! Diana is very good at liking people. Every day, Diana inspires me. I used to think I just wanted to know as much stuff as she knows – and as many people, if that's even possible."

There was laughter at this.

"I thought that I could be like her... I tried to be clever and I ended up looking like an idiot. Now I know that the best way for me to be more like Diana is by trying to be a better person. I encourage you all to try it. Let's sing her a round of Happy Birthday, shall we?"

Zaf led the singing, and they all raised a glass to Diana.

"It's alright, Diana, we won't give you the bumps!" Zaf shouted.

More applause.

The bear-like bulk of Detective Chief Inspector Clint Sugarbrook appeared at Diana's side.

"For a moment there, I thought he was going to do a Diana Bakewell."

"*Do a Diana Bakewell?*" she said.

"You know. Make a wild accusation that so-and-so killed so-and-so."

Diana laughed politely. "Thank you for coming, by the way."

On stage, Zaf made to give the microphone back, hesitated, and then garbled, "Tom Hatcher killed David Medawar."

There was silence from the crowd, interspersed with gasps of surprise from a few people.

"And there we go," sighed Sugarbrook. "He gets it from you."

"Um, yes," said Zaf. "Thought I'd put it out there, not because I've just discovered Tom is... Never mind that. And, yes, now that I think about it, unmasking a murderer at a birthday barbecue is not a 'better person' thing to do."

Diana watched his face. He was making a fool of himself, and he knew it.

Zaf licked his lips. "But he did. He killed David Medawar."

"This is outrageous!" shouted Tom from the marquee, sounding more amused than offended.

The bridge fans were there, and the bulk of the hen party too. Diana could see they were unsure whether Zaf was being serious, or if this was just more entertainment.

"Excuse me," Diana said to Sugarbrook. She pushed forward through the crowd. "Excuse me! Birthday girl coming through!"

She reached the stage and got up beside Zaf. He surrendered the microphone to her. Diana turned to her audience.

"Thank you. And can we thank Zaf for his kind and only slightly bewildering words." She clapped, and the party guests dutifully followed suit.

"It has been a pleasure to have Zaf as a colleague, housemate and friend. And it's a sheer joy to see so many friends, new and old, gathered here."

She might have left it at that. But something compelled her to go on.

"David Medawar was a customer of ours," she said. "He was on a tour two days ago and he died while our bus was crossing Tower Bridge." She frowned. "He died somewhere on our journey before we got to the far side of Tower Bridge. He was strangled."

There were gasps, downcast looks and solemn nods, especially among the bridge chaps.

"I found his body," Diana said. "Zaf was with me soon after. We didn't know the man. No one here really knew him. The only real clue he left behind was an Agatha Christie novel and a note in which he'd written two lines. *Check the Pale Horse* and *Cat at Tower not in diary*. Cryptic stuff."

She gestured to Zaf.

"Zaf, you said Tom killed him."

"Er, I did."

"That's slander and lies," shouted Tom.

Diana scanned the crowd and fixed him with a hard stare. "Be careful, Tom, about accusing people of being liars. You yourself are a liar. You admitted as much."

"I did?"

"You claimed to be a gifted actor and liar. Those very words. You were happy to feign sadness at David's passing."

"I didn't know him."

"You didn't. He was just an investor in your Bifrost bridge project."

"Exactly."

"But he'd come all the way to London to talk to you. 'A difficult conversation,' as someone had described it. David was far from happy."

"Are you actually accusing our Tom here?" called out Stuart Dinktrout.

"I absolutely am accusing him," said Diana, putting a hand on Zaf's back.

Chapter Fifty-One

Zaf watched Tom's face while Diana spoke. It was set in a fixed expression of cautious watchfulness, as if he was waiting for the whole horrible truth to come out.

"Several people saw David in the hotel on the night before he died," Diana said. "One of our guests, Bethan, had visited him in his room and, according to witnesses, was heard crying as she left."

This drew gasps from the hen party.

One of them elbowed Bethan in the ribs. "You sly dog, Bethan Griffiths."

"But after that conversation, David's demeanour was described as angry," Diana said. "Tom had met David by that point and Tom had told him that 'it' – whatever 'it' was – was not worth crying over."

Zaf surveyed the crowd. Everyone was silent and attentive. However little they understood about the whole story, they all wanted to hear how it ended.

"David wasn't interested in bridges," Diana went on, her

hand still on Zaf's back. "He was no engineer. He was a chemist, in fact, and a man with a keen analytical mind. A reader of mysteries. I wish I'd got to know him. He only knew the other people on our bridge tour because he had invested in it. And while he was in London, he crassly asked another investor how much money he'd put into the project."

"He did," said Stuart.

"David Medawar realised he had been betrayed. He had been cheated. He had been robbed. Because Tom Hatcher is a liar and David Medawar had worked it all out. That's why he wrote *Cat at Tower not in diary*."

Zaf gestured to take the microphone. Diana passed it over.

"I worked that out," he said. "I mean, I'm sure Diana worked it out too. Probably before me. We realised that the *Cat at Tower* diary thing was about Catherine Garratt at Tower Division Engineering. Those are the people Tom was supposed to be selling his bridge thing too. But, you see, we thought that the diary must have referred to the diary of our guest, Gaynor—"

"Whoo! Gaynor!" hollered one of the hens, as if Zaf were doing call-outs at a stage show.

"But it wasn't," said Zaf. "The diary wasn't Gaynor's. It was Catherine Garratt's. Cat at Tower Division had nothing in her diary." He looked at Tom. "That meeting we hurried to get to yesterday. There was no meeting, was there?"

Tom stared, silent.

"You just told people you had a meeting," Zaf said. "Your friends and investors knew you'd struggled to get the prototypes working. The bolt fired from the Bifrost system could rarely find purchase in the ground when it was fired."

"Terrain's tricky," Newton called out helpfully.

"Meanwhile, Tom was running out of money. Bunty said as much."

"Did I?" said Bunty.

"Two million pounds from investors," said Diana. "You took their money and had nothing to show for it, except a pretty-looking model."

"Form without function," added Zaf. "If the thing doesn't work, what's the point of it?"

"So what did you do?" Diana said. "You threw a celebratory weekend away and faked a meeting to assure them everything was on track—"

"—and then you were planning to run away to Spain with the rest of the money!" Zaf continued, feeling his chest tighten. "Where you have a secret wife, too!"

Diana lowered her voice. "Let's not get side-tracked here."

"But he does!" Zaf whispered.

"Sorry, gents," Diana said to the tour party, "but your leader has been stringing you along. He has taken your cash, and there is no military super-bridge money coming back to you. David Medawar worked it out. He must have had some suspicion, perhaps he called Tower Division Engineering. He was angry, and had every right to be."

"So that's why Tom killed him?" asked a woman from the hen party.

Zaf was about to nod. But Diana said, "No. I don't think he did. He could have. He had the opportunity and the motive, but I don't think he did."

"He didn't?" said Zaf.

Diana shook her head.

Zaf looked over the crowd. If they'd been confused before, they were doubly so now.

"But the note," he said. "The lies. It all makes sense. I thought we were accusing him."

"Of fraud," she said. "That's his crime."

"Is this true?" Bunty turned to the spot where Tom had been.

Tom wasn't there. He was already through the crowd, heading for the gates into the square, and only impeded by the broad and unnavigable torso of DCI Sugarbrook. He stopped, shoulders slumped.

"So who did kill him?" called Gaynor Griffiths.

Diana smiled. "Gaynor, did you know, I thought it was you."

Chapter Fifty-Two

Gaynor looked stunned. Diana felt ashamed; she was making an ill woman suffer further.

"It had occurred to me that you had something of a motive for killing David Medawar."

"What motive?" Gaynor asked.

Diana stepped to the front of the little stage. "You met David Medawar the night before he died. Tom saw you and Bethan talking to him in the hotel restaurant. I think the three of you were chatting for a long time."

"We were. So?"

"We know Bethan went to his room later. Whatever the reason was, it didn't end happily for Bethan."

"I wasn't crying," Bethan said.

"One thing I've learned over this weekend, Gaynor," Diana said, "is that you care and have always cared for your daughters."

"Of course I have!"

"You're very protective of them."

"I am!"

"And you know that Bethan has not exactly been lucky when it comes to finding Mr Right."

"Please," said Bethan. "Can we not do this here?"

Diana pressed on. "That broken arm. How did you do it?"

"I ran into a lamppost!"

"A spiral fracture like that? And you admitted that Daryl was too fond of the drink."

"I don't see why I should have to fight to make you believe me!"

Diana pursed her lips. "It's easy to see why Gaynor feels protective of you, the one daughter who has stayed by her side to care for her all this time."

"Hey!" shouted Arwen. "I love my mum, I do!"

"We even saw," said Diana, pointing towards Borough, eastward and across the river, "that you were prepared to fight to protect Bethan from the attentions of young men at the wine bar."

"I'd had a bit to drink is all," said Gaynor.

"What wouldn't a mother do to protect a daughter who had been offended, who had been threatened by whatever David Medawar had subjected her to that night in the hotel?"

Arwen looked at her mum. "Did you strangle that man, Mum?"

"No," said Gaynor. "No!"

"No," agreed Diana. "No, you didn't kill him, though for a while that seemed the most obvious answer to me."

"So, do you know who *did* kill him?" Bunty called out.

"Let's not go making any more wild and crazy accusations," cautioned DCI Sugarbrook, who was also trying to supervise a pair of young girls holding ketchup-covered hotdogs.

"Do you actually know who killed him?" Zaf whispered next to her on the stage.

"I *do* know who killed him," Diana said, loud enough for all to hear. "The business with the crying in the corridor is very much the key to it all. As is David Medawar's cryptic note on that piece of paper. It's all about a diary."

"What diary?" asked Bunty.

"Gaynor's diary." Diana gestured to the mother of the bride.

"Really?" said Gaynor.

"It's a diary that's been the focus of a lot of attention. It was lost at one point and then found again. It's very important indeed."

"I don't think so," said Gaynor. "It's just my day-to-day things. Nothing scandalous in there."

"Ah," said Diana, with a warning look at Zaf, "but what one person reads in a diary is entirely different from what someone else might read in the same diary."

"Alright," he whispered. "I'm sorry."

"Old boyfriend indeed," she muttered. She raised her voice again. "Gaynor, your diary is what this whole business has been about, and I didn't know for certain until DCI Sugarbrook told me what had been used to strangle David Medawar. Your diary, if we're lucky, might just save a life."

Diana could feel the intensity of everyone's gaze now. It was time to lay it all out.

"David Medawar came to the Redhouse Hotel on Thursday. He joined our tour group in order to level an accusation of fraud against Tom Hatcher. It was by pure chance that he ended up talking to Gaynor and Bethan Griffiths in the restaurant bar. Bethan said he showed a polite and courteous interest in Gaynor's illness and that Gaynor spoke at length about her condition."

"He was a very polite man," said Gaynor.

"I imagine so. He had an enquiring mind. Nose always in a book. In fact, later that evening, Stuart saw him going to the lifts, studying a hardback book. He didn't recognise that it was a diary. It was your diary, wasn't it, Gaynor?"

"He asked to borrow it," she said, arms folded across her chest. "There was nothing in there so personal I wouldn't let someone else read it."

"Bit odd," said Diana, nose wrinkling. "A man wanting to read someone else's diary. If it's about your illness then it might be understandable if he was a doctor, an oncologist. But he wasn't. He was a... what was it?"

"He worked in chemicals," Zaf said.

"That's it. He knew chemicals. And he knew murder mysteries. He wrote on the bookmark in the book found next to his body *Check the Pale Horse,* which is an Agatha Christie novel. And we know he wrote that on Thursday evening or Friday morning because the stationery was a piece of hotel letter-headed paper.'"

"And that's got something to do with my diary, has it?" said Gaynor.

"David thought so," Diana replied. "Because he knew chemicals and he knew that Agatha Christie knew chemicals. Didn't you say to me, Gaynor, that someone had told you real life murders had been solved because the police saw similarities between them and Mrs Christie's novels?"

"Er... yes."

"But you don't remember *who* told you that?"

"No?"

"Was it David Medawar by any chance?"

The eyes framed by that bold brassy wig blinked. "I don't know."

"David saw something crucial in that diary, a clue that no one else had spotted, not even you, Gaynor, who wrote it. And that's why the murderer stole the diary."

Diana saw confusion on several faces. "To be clear, David returned the diary to Gaynor the next morning but then, later that day, it was stolen from Gaynor's bag while we were all cooped up together in the function room. We have the photographic evidence to prove it."

"No, I found it again," Gaynor said. "I'd just dropped it in my room."

"That was where it was found again," Diana corrected her. "The murderer stole it but the diary was found again, much to the killer's surprise."

"But what was in the diary?" asked Arwen.

"Evidence of attempted murder. A long, long account of a murder that was about to be completed."

"David's murder?" said Gaynor.

"No, Gaynor," said Diana. "Yours."

Chapter Fifty-Three

"My murder?" Gaynor's pale face was slack with surprise. "I'm... I'm not dead."

"No. But you have been poisoned."

Gaynor stared at the glass of fizz in her hand.

Diana shook her head. "There's this chemical, a heavy metal. Thallium. It's the murderer's weapon of choice in the Agatha Christie novel, *The Pale Horse*. And, importantly, a side effect of thallium poisoning is hair loss."

Gaynor's hand rose to her wig. "I have Hodgkin Lymphoma. This isn't funny."

"No, it's not. And I assume you did have Hodgkin Lymphoma at some point. And I'm guessing that, although you're unaware of the fact, you don't have it any more. The treatments worked. You were cured."

"That's a lie," said Bethan. "It can't be..."

"It's been pointed out to me that the hospital appointments just stopped. No more letters inviting you to appointments. But no all-clear letters, either."

"I have cancer," Gaynor insisted.

"Are you just making all this up?" Arwen said.

"You can't know this," Bethan added.

Diana looked at the two daughters. "There was a point at which your mum was dying, and then there came a point when she was not. We learn to accept certain things, even make plans around them and then, when the situation changes... I imagine that might be quite annoying."

"Me staying alive is annoying?" Gaynor said.

"After a fashion," Diana replied. "You told me that, when you were gone, you'd have nothing to leave your daughters but a big old empty house. The thing is, big old empty houses are valuable things."

Gaynor shook her head. "This is horrible. Baseless accusations. I didn't write anything in my diary about thallium. I don't even know what that is. What could that man have spotted?"

"David spotted a change that showed you were being poisoned, increment by increment."

"What change?"

"You told me. Twice."

"What change?" Gaynor demanded.

"You felt better. You improved."

"So?"

"Two weeks. That's what you said. Over the course of two weeks, you felt better. Your decline eased. That's what David spotted. It only took a few questions for him to work out why."

Gaynor looked confused.

"Arwen was wrapped up in her wedding plans," Diana continued, "and Bethan laid up with a broken arm. You were left alone and in that window, you began to feel better. Bethan, you went to David's room the night before he died."

Bethan hesitated. "We just talked. Nothing happened between us."

"I believe you," said Diana. "You spoke almost exclusively about your mum's illness and the inconsistencies in her health as recorded in that diary. David, the chemist, suspected thallium poisoning, and I think he told you that. That would have been very upsetting for you to hear. You left his room and were heard sobbing."

"You knew about this?" said Gaynor.

"Don't listen to her," replied Bethan.

"He had, through ingenuity and guesswork, hit upon the truth," said Diana. "A truth he would have probably shared with you, Gaynor, if he'd not been killed the following day."

"What even is this poison?" said Gaynor.

"It's a heavy metal element. Tasteless, hard to detect in the body. It was once commonly used as a rat poison, but it's too toxic for people to handle. These days it has a number of specific industrial uses. I had to look them up. One of those is the manufacture of imitation jewellery."

Gaynor and Arwen looked as one at Bethan.

"No," Gaynor whispered.

Bethan was frozen, transfixed.

"Arwen told me that Bethan worked with some pretty nasty chemicals but it was you, Bethan, who told DCI Sugarbrook in the interview that you are in charge of stocktaking at your company's factory."

"Why?" said Gaynor, her face even paler than usual.

"Those gambling debts," said Diana. "What you described as Bethan's addictive personality. I think she's in debt to the kind of people who might send someone to break her arm and deliver a very specific message."

Bethan cradled her broken arm.

"And it was when Detective Sugarbrook mentioned fibres in the wound earlier today that I remembered meeting Bethan on Friday, wearing a sling that disappeared later in the day. I can imagine that once David was dead you threw it aside for the wind to take, to go fluttering into the Thames or somewhere."

"No," said Bethan, shaking her head.

"For months, you've been micro-dosing your mum with thallium. You loved your mum, but you'd accepted the Hodgkin Lymphoma would kill her. And the money from the inheritance would be compensation for the months and months of care you'd provided. I can imagine how shocked, offended even, you might have felt to discover that she was going to be fine."

"No," Bethan repeated.

"And when you spoke to David and he revealed his suspicion that your mum was being poisoned, you were of course distraught and afraid. I might feel the same in your situation. I might feel desperate enough to kill the man the next day, when a chance arose on the top of a double-decker bus. And I might even steal the diary, conceal it from anyone else who might spot the same pattern. Although I would probably find a better place to hide it than under my bed in the room I was sharing with my mum."

Sugarbrook had made his way through the silent crowd with his daughters. He stood behind Gaynor. Tom stood mutely behind him, his attempt to flee forgotten in the tension of the moment.

"Detective Chief Inspector," Diana said, "if Gaynor has her 'nutritious' smoothie on her, you might want to take it for analysis. And Gaynor, you might need to go to a hospital. You are, as you say, very ill."

Chapter Fifty-Four

Zaf loved a party. And he'd been to more than one party where the police had turned up, blue lights flashing, to break things up and restore the peace.

But this was the first party he'd been at where one attendee was arrested for murder, another arrested for fraud, a third hurried to hospital, and more than a dozen others went off in various states of fury and distress, leaving the stunned residents of Eccleston Square to wonder if all of Diana Bakewell's birthdays were like this.

"This party ain't over yet," said Big Ernie. He stabbed a button on the sound system, which did absolutely nothing.

"Blasted thing!" he declared, and fiddled with it. "You all get some food while I figure this out. There's still plenty of sausages."

People did as they were told and as Zaf stood there, he heard the sound of a guitar playing.

He looked around and saw that Gus had heard it too. The soft grey tabby cat was sashaying through the marquee in search of the music. Zaf followed.

He came to the foot of a small fountain, where Alexsei Dadashov sat.

"Sorry," Zaf mumbled, worried that he was intruding.

Alexsei looked up in silence. The strumming picked up tempo, an impassioned Spanish flamenco sound. Alexsei treated him to a full ten seconds of intense playing before settling back to a gentle rhythm.

"Is it normal to bring a cat to a party?" Alexsei asked.

Zaf looked down. Gus was pushing up against his calves while running a figure of eight through his legs.

"It's not my cat."

"No," Alexsei agreed. "Cats do not belong to anyone. That was a good speech."

"Which part? The bit where I accused a man of murder or... actually I can't remember what I blathered on about in the other part."

Alexsei did a little flourish and stopped playing. He smiled at Zaf.

"You reminded us that you think yourself a fool. But that some of us like you just the way you are, and that you like us back. That was nice to hear."

"Thank you. I mean, good."

Alexsei didn't break eye contact. Zaf felt a sudden awkwardness.

He took a breath. "You *are* off with me sometimes."

Alexsei raised an eyebrow. "Excuse me?"

"Alexsei Dadashov, you are sometimes *off* with me. And judgemental. Haughty. That's the word. The way you look at me, like I'm..."

Alexsei was looking at him right now with a powerful intensity.

"But you really are a nice person," Zaf stuttered, "a nice

man, and I think I do like you and I would like to like you more than I do. I..." He grunted at himself. "I'm a tour guide. I should be great with words. What I'm trying to say, badly, is that despite all the awkwardness and that, I would like to like you more than I do."

Alexsei gave him a lopsided smile. "I would like that too."

Zaf opened his mouth to reply but was interrupted by the sound of dance music, followed by a cheer from all the hidden corners of the garden park.

Gus jumped onto Alexsei's lap. He nudged Alexsei's hand, resting on the guitar strings. The cat's head produced a discordant and muffled sound against the strings.

"I'd best get back..." Zaf pointed a thumb towards the party.

"I am currently trapped under a cat," Alexsei said, stroking Gus's head. "I will be along shortly."

Zaf nodded.

"It occurs to me," said Alexsei as Zaf turned to go, "that Bryan's flat on the top floor is empty."

"Yes?"

"I live on the ground floor."

"You do."

"And I will not just be renting out that flat to whichever person makes the highest offer. If they are going to be my neighbour, I would like to vet them carefully. This will take time."

"Quite possibly."

"In the meantime, there would be no problem if you decided to live there."

Zaf gasped. "I can have Bryan's flat?"

A shrug. "Until I rent it out to someone else. It might be a good thing if Diana – or you – want a little privacy."

Zaf was stunned. "You are the most strange and surprising man, Mr Dadashov."

He turned and skipped away. Actually skipped.

Was it because of the offer of a free flat? Or because of the 'I like you just as you are'?

He didn't know. He didn't care.

He entered the marquee and felt a touch at his elbow: Diana.

"I was coming to look for you," he said.

"You've found me."

"I really did need to say thank you."

"For what?"

He pulled a face. "For leaping in when I started randomly accusing Tom Hatcher of murder?"

Diana gave him an amused smile. "Oh, he was a wrong 'un. You knew that as well as I did. He just didn't kill David Medawar."

"He had a reason to, of a sort."

"And maybe the opportunity. But it turns out an even more desperate person got there first." She swept her arms round at the gathered friends – mingling, dancing, laughing – and the golden glow of fairy lights against the London night. "This is lovely, isn't it?"

"It really is. And we can do it all again next year."

"Although maybe check with me before inviting any surprise guests next time."

"Sorry."

She gave his arm a playful nudge. "It was, I suppose, a nice surprise in the end."

"Good," said Zaf. "And yes."

"Yes?"

"I'll check with you before inviting surprise guests. We

wouldn't want there to be any surprises at a birthday party, would we?"

"Absolutely not."

"Now, I think I need a drink and a sit down."

"Drinks are over here," she said and put her arm through his to lead the way.

Read a free story, Gus the Theatre Cat

Gus the tabby cat is now a firm fixture at Chartwell and Crouch Bus Tours. Newton the bus driver has taken him under his wing and regularly provides him with cans of tuna. And the tour guides Diana and Zaf are finding he's a hit with the guests.

But then when Diana and Zaf are showing a group of theatre professionals around London, Gus disappears in a West End theatre.

Newton is distraught. He's searched the theatre high and low but can't find his beloved feline friend.

One night, when Diana and Zaf are watching the performance, he has a plan. It involves plenty of cunning, a fair amount of sneaking around in the auditorium and quite a lot of tinned tuna.

Can Newton find Gus without causing total chaos for the audience?

Find out in this London Cozy Mysteries short story.

Read *Gus the Theatre Cat* for FREE at rachelmclean.com/gus.

Read the London Cosy Mysteries Series

Death at Westminster

Death in the West End

Death at Tower Bridge

Death on the Thames

...and more to come

Buy from book retailers or via the Rachel McLean website.

Also by Rachel McLean

The DI Zoe Finch Series – buy from book retailers or via the Rachel McLean website.

Deadly Wishes

Deadly Choices

Deadly Desires

Deadly Terror

Deadly Reprisal

Deadly Fallout

Deadly Christmas

Deadly Origins, the FREE Zoe Finch prequel

The Dorset Crime Series – buy from book retailers or via the Rachel McLean website.

The Corfe Castle Murders

The Clifftop Murders

The Island Murders

The Monument Murders

The Millionaire Murders

The Fossil Beach Murders

The Fossil Beach Murders

The Blue Pool Murders

The Lighthouse Murders

The Ghost Village Murders

The McBride & Tanner Series – Buy from book retailers or via the Rachel McLean website.

Blood and Money

Death and Poetry

Power and Treachery

...and more to come

The Cumbria Crime Series by Rachel McLean and Joel Hames – Buy from book retailers or via the Rachel McLean website.

The Harbour

The Mine

The Cairn

...and more to come

Also by Millie Ravensworth

The Cozy Craft Mysteries – Buy now in ebook and paperback

The Wonderland Murders

The Painted Lobster Murders

The Sequinned Cape Murders

The Swan Dress Murders

The Tie-Dyed Kaftan Murders

The Scarecrow Murders

Printed in Great Britain
by Amazon